AND WITH MADNESS COMES THE LIGHT

AN EXPERIMENT IN TERROR NOVELLA #6.5

KARINA HALLE

Copyright © 2012 by Karina Halle

First edition published by Metal Blonde Books

Second edition published 2020

All rights reserved.

No part of this book may be reproduced in any form or by any electronic or mechanical means, including information storage and retrieval systems, without written permission from the author, except for the use of brief quotations in a book review.

Cover: Hang Le Designs

For Scott – I knew Dex before I knew you but you won the spot in my heart

ONE

"I was head over heels in love with her. No, that didn't describe it. I was tear my fucking heart out and throw it at her, beg her to take it into hers. I was falling from the greatest heights with no safety net below. I was giving everything of my own life for hers, giving up every inch of my soul so she could wear it proudly. I was a former king on my knees in front of the queen. A jester begging for a chance. I was powerless, helpless, and at her mercy."

THERE'S NOTHING MORE FRIGHTENING THAN THE DAWN that seems darker than the night. When you wait for hours for that first glimpse of daylight, the constant reminder that our planet is turning and life does go on, and you get only darkness instead. Maybe the sun is out there, somewhere, and maybe the world keeps rolling on, but fuck if I knew it. All I could see was this darkness, this black oblivion that sucked me dry until I was nothing but a husk of my former self. There was no light in all this madness. My tattoo was a lie.

The morning after Perry left me—after I created this hole—the sun never came up. I spent the night tossing and turning on the bed in the den until I couldn't stand the smell of her hair on the sheets. Somehow I made it to the couch, and somehow, when I eventually awoke, I wasn't alone.

I wished I was.

"Dex." Jenn's voice broke into the abyss.

I didn't want to face her. Last night, she found me crying on the floor. She helped me up, and for the first time ever, took care of me. Maybe because the guilt she was carrying matched my own. Maybe because that was the last time she'd have to and she was saving the best for last.

I opened my eyes slowly. The room was grey, monotonous, dead. She was sitting in the armchair she had pulled up in front of me, the one she hated because I bought it at IKEA. She looked just as awful as I did, which made me even sadder. When Jennifer Rodriguez resembles a pufferfish with extensions you know something terrible has gone down.

"Dex, we need to talk," she said, her voice hoarse. She looked down at her knees, clad in silky pajama bottoms, her wild hair obscuring her eyes.

Usually those words make any man sit up. Perhaps even jump out the window. I was too hollow, too weak, too blank to do anything except lie there and watch her. She looked different, the room looked different, nothing would ever be the same. And though I could have found some respite in that, this change meant losing Perry as well. And therefore, it meant nothing.

"So talk," I told her, because I didn't have the strength

to do it myself. Besides, I wanted to hear it from her own mouth. I wanted to hear her finally admit her mistakes. I wanted—more than anything—the chance to admit mine.

She began running her lacquered nails up and down her legs, creating lines on her pants that slowly faded in the silk. This was hard for her. I took some comfort in that.

"I...," she said and looked up, away from me. Her eyes glistened with tears. If I could have cared, I would have. No one wants to see a woman cry, even a twatwaffling she-devil. "I think we need to break up."

I kept my gaze steady on her. "You don't say."

She sniffed and gently wiped under her eyes, as if she'd mess up the nonexistent makeup she was wearing. "I haven't been fair to you. And I know you haven't been fair to me."

My eyes narrowed. "How haven't I been fair?"

She looked at me sharply. "You're in love with another woman."

"And you're in love with another man. How long have you and Sir Douche, I mean Bradley, been going on for?"

She slid over the insult with ease. "How long have you and Perry been going on for?"

I jerked a little. "It's not like that."

"Yeah, well, I guess you win then," she said, pulling her hair off her face. She really was such a beautiful girl. No wonder I had been blind for so long. She had ways of making you feel like the luckiest man on earth, just because you were seen together. She made you wonder, *why me?* But I knew why. Because I was safe too. We both used each other as a safety net until the holes got too big.

And I definitely wasn't the winner here. Not by a longshot.

"So, if we're both being honest for once, tell me...how long?" I repeated.

She let out a pained sigh. "Since...since you left Wine Babes. Since you left me."

I really didn't want to get pulled into another argument over my departure; all of that shit was a moot point now. And, surprisingly enough, it didn't sting as much as I thought it would. I guess my pride really had been demolished during the night.

"Why didn't you just end it?" I asked.

She shrugged. "Why didn't you?"

"Because..." I began. Then I couldn't find the words. I was afraid. I was afraid to take a chance with Perry for a million different reasons. I was afraid to get hurt. I was afraid to lose my heart, my soul, my everything, for a woman who might not have wanted me back. For someone I needed more than anything.

"I didn't know how she felt," I said quietly, staring at the carpet.

She snorted. "Right. Dex, that girl was head over heels in love with you. And you were in love with her. I knew it from the moment she walked into this apartment. You looked at her in a way that you've never looked at me. And she looked at you in the way I never did. You could have done this properly, you know."

"I'm sorry we can't all fuck other people behind each other's back," I snarled.

She crossed her legs and folded her hands together, the Latino bite coming back. "Right. Okay, Dex. Like you didn't fuck her here last night."

"It was just once," I told her, hiding a white lie.

"I can see that. It's not my fault that you had to screw it all up after."

Actually it kind of was. "You cheated on me constantly."

She leaned forward so her puffy eyes were just inches away. "And so did you. I may have been screwing Bradley with my body but you were fucking Perry with your heart. And which one is worse, huh?"

I bit down on my lip until I tasted blood. Finally, I said, "There's nothing worse than that."

She nodded, a flash of open vulnerability on her face. "We both screwed up."

"We sure did."

"I guess we couldn't just break up like normal people."

I managed a smile. "Jenn, you know I'm not normal."

She smiled back, wistful. "I know." She reached over and grabbed my hand, giving it a quick squeeze. It would be the last time Jenn would ever touch me.

Later that day, she made plans to move in with Bradley. She decided to leave Fat Rabbit behind since the dog always liked me better anyway, and Metro Von Dickfucker had an apparent allergy to dogs. She packed up her ugly cheetah-print suitcase, told me she'd be back in a couple of days to get the rest of her stuff, and wished me luck.

I needed all the luck I could get.

The next few days before Jenn came to get her stuff were an absolute write-off. Rebecca kept calling me and I kept thinking about calling Perry. I wouldn't answer anyone's calls, and Perry wouldn't answer mine. I couldn't eat, I couldn't shit. I drank myself into a stupor, and the only time I left the apartment was to take Fat Rabbit out around the block. The rest of the time, I just left the balcony door open and the little bastard did his business out there. I was too empty inside to care if our apartment was turning into Turd City.

I'm not one to wallow in self-pity, really I'm not. The last time I did that, I ended up in a mental institution on extremely strong drugs, pining after Abby, a girl who would later turn up dead. And then, years later, end up in my apartment. Still dead.

The funny thing was I expected to see Abby haunting me now that Perry and Jenn were gone. I expected to see her grotesque form gliding down the hallway or hanging suspended from the bedroom ceiling. I expected to see her standing amidst Turd City's shitbrick buildings, beckoning me with her finger.

But Abby never came. And, to be honest, I was kind of disappointed. How fucking lonely was I, to be craving the company of a deranged ghost? No, this time I was so completely and utterly alone. I had no one but a smelly dog, and even he was starting to resent me for the deteriorating conditions.

I just didn't see the point in anything. While my thoughts weren't exactly suicidal, I entertained the idea of ending it all. I knew I would never do it, but I fantasized about how easy it would be. How no one would care. And how quickly the pain would stop. I didn't want to die but I didn't want to live either. Living, breathing, existing from day to day only added to the weight on my heart.

Shut the fuck up, man. Get over it. Shape up or ship out. Don't think I wasn't yelling those things in my head. But when the fuck did my head and heart get along anyway? They were mortal enemies now, sworn to rip each other to shreds.

I fucked up. More than I have ever fucked up before. I

had the love of my life in my hands for one beautiful, exquisite moment before I ripped her apart and my heart bore the paper cuts. Perry…I'd never see her smiling face again. I'd never hear her melodic voice. I'd never be able to make her laugh or cringe or yell at me. God damn it, even if she would pick up her phone, scream at me, and give me eternal hell for the way I acted after we slept together, it would make me whole again. But there was nothing but silence. Nothing but darkness.

It took Jenn and Fuckface barging in the apartment while I was sleeping (okay, so it was the middle of the day), to bring me out of my first funk. Jenn ran in the room waving her arms above her head like a muppet, screaming at me over the state of the apartment, and threatening to call the SPCA for Fat Rabbit. I knew she was right. And when I heard the disappointed noises from Bradley in the living room, I realized I still had a smoldering coal of pride left in me. Abercrombie & Douche wasn't going to get both my ex-girlfriend and a coat of self-righteousness.

"Jenn," I said, sitting up in bed. She was looking around the room like I'd hidden shit everywhere. Literal shit. "Make this quick."

"You're disgusting," she announced, flouncing over to a half-eaten pizza on the floor. "What the fuck happened?"

"You know what happened," I said quietly, surprised at the embarrassment I was feeling, relieved that it meant I was alive. "I lost everything."

She stopped in the middle of the room, slender hands on slender hips. "You lost nothing you didn't already have."

"How many negatives were in that sentence?" I asked, trying to count them.

She rolled her eyes, still managing to look disgusted.

"You can't lose something you never owned to begin with. Accept that and move on."

"Whoa," I said, shaking my head. "How fast you've gone to Bitch Town. Where's the compassion I saw in you the other day?"

"I only have so much. You've used it all up."

"So, this is how it's going to be?" I asked, almost amused by her coldness.

"Jenn," Bradley yelled from the living room, "maybe we should come back after we call the hazmat team."

"Great idea," I yelled back. "They can spray you both down for your crotch rot while they're at it."

"Real mature," she sniped, edging toward the door.

"Someone has to be."

Her green eyes narrowed into feline slits. "I'll come back in two days, Dex. Noon. I expect you'll not only be out of the apartment so I don't have to see your dirty mug, but that it will be clean and all my stuff will be stacked by the door. If not, I really will call somebody about this."

I didn't know who she'd call aside from the SPCA, but I wasn't going to risk it. I glared back at her as a way of conceding. I didn't want to just do as she said—obviously—and that coal of pride was starting to flame. I'd show both of them.

I started by taking the longest shower of my life, followed by the longest jerk-off session of my life. I thought of Perry's ample ass the entire time I was beating it, and I'm happy to say I didn't shed a single tear. Of course, in my fantasy, none of this shit ever happened.

Then came the cleaning of the apartment, which I'm not sure how I handled. No wonder they were so disgusted —I'd seen better living conditions under the Pine I-5 overpass. Finally, I started answering my phone when it rang. I got one hell of a lashing from Rebecca once I told her what had happened between Perry and me.

She wasted no time in giving me that lashing in person. *Crack.*

Rebecca's hand flew across my face the minute I opened the door. She didn't even look, she just walked in and *smack*. It was almost scary, like she had some preternatural slapping ability. Maybe all Brits had that.

"You fucking wanker!" she yelled at me, throwing her purse on the kitchen counter. "You piece of shit, good for nothing, pathetic excuse for a man."

I stroked my chin and looked her up and down. She looked like some '40s femme fatale with her smooth black hair, red lips, and sculpted dress. She seethed like one, too.

"You're quite attractive when you're indignant," I commented.

Smack. Again. Man, she was fast.

My cheek stung as I rubbed at it. I shot her a wary glance and backed away. "Are you done now?"

"No," she said, folding her arms and tapping her pumps. "No, I'm not done. I'm just getting started. How dare you?"

"I know," I mumbled and dragged myself over to the couch. Fat Rabbit glared at me as I sat beside him, still mad over the neglect.

She stood where she was, which made things a little less frightening. "You slept with Perry and broke up with her right after. I can't think of a more...selfish, cowardly thing to do. What's wrong with you?!"

"Okay, well first of all, we weren't going out so I didn't break up with her."

"Semantics, asshole. Semantics and excuses. You knew how she felt about you."

I pointed my finger at her, suddenly defensive. "No!

No, I did not. She lied to me; she told me she didn't love me."

"And you believed her?"

I threw my hands up. "Of course I believed her! She's my best friend. She was. We trusted each other. I asked her if she loved me, and she said no. To my face. She lied. Why wouldn't I have believed her?"

She let out a puff of air as her thoughts ran amok. "I don't know. Because it was so obvious to everyone."

"Everyone except me! Why would I think she loved me anyway? And why would I assume she lied? When Perry tells me something, I believe her. I hardly think that's the most jackassery thing I could do."

She lowered her chin. "She loved you, Dex."

Another fucking blow to my motherfucking heart. I was surprised it hadn't been pulverized to dust by now.

"Maybe she did, maybe she didn't," I said, not wanting to think about it. "I guess it doesn't really matter now."

She walked over to me, heels clicking on the floor, and elegantly sat beside me. I caught a whiff of flowers.

"Dex," she said softly, placing her delicate hand on my shoulder until I was forced to meet her eyes. "Do you love Perry?"

The thing I could no longer ignore. There was no point in hiding it now.

"Yes," I told her, looking her straight on, my heart banging in my chest. "I love her, more than anyone should love anything. The kind of love that either fills you up or eats away at you. I love her at my own risk. I love her…dangerously."

We elapsed into silence for a few loaded moments before she gave my shoulder a squeeze. "I know you do."

"Then why did you ask?"

"Because I wanted you to say it. It's not real until you do."

"Also," I went on, ignoring her, "if you knew she loved me, and I loved her, why didn't you say something to us?"

She shook her head, not willing to take the blame. "It wasn't my part. This isn't high school. You're adults. If you're meant to come together it will be through your actions, not someone else's."

"Oh, how philosophical."

"It's the truth. And it's not over yet between you two."

"Right." I laughed sharply. "Every email I send, every phone call I make, goes unanswered. She doesn't even have her voicemail anymore. She probably changed her number. She's cut me off and cut me off forever."

"Maybe for now," she said. "And maybe she needs to. But forever is more fickle than you think."

Forget fickle, forever was a bitch.

TWO

Two days later, just as she'd threatened, Jenn and Bradley returned. For everyone's sake, I was gone, taking Fat Rabbit to a dive bar down the street that I knew wouldn't bat an eye at the fact that it was noon, nor the fact that I had a dog with me. I'd been going there every day since I started wearing pants again, so I was good for business.

I smoked cigarette after cigarette (another thing they let me do when it wasn't too busy) and drank JD after glass of JD. The bartender—a wiry fellow with ugly star tattoos on his neck—kept them coming until it was time for me to return home.

The minute I stepped back in the apartment, woozy on my feet, thanks to my shit eating habits, and wet from Seattle's relentless December downpours, I was slammed with a sense of finality. Like, fuck—this was real. This was over. This was my life now.

The apartment looked stripped to the bones. Half the art was gone, half the furniture was gone. I was left with the couch, the IKEA chair plus the TV on the ground—she'd taken the coffee table, entertainment unit, even the shitty rug. Who the fuck takes back a rug?

I dropped Fat Rabbit's leash and stumbled to the bedroom. Thank god the bed was there, though I didn't see why she'd need the end tables. Of course she wouldn't need them. Jenn took them out of spite. As if fucking around with dickass the whole time wasn't enough for her. She got to walk away with the love—or fuck—of her life while I was left with nothing. Rebecca had been thrilled when I told her that Jenn and I finally broke up, but I just couldn't share that sentiment. Not now. Not when I felt like I'd been robbed of the life I once had. Happy or not, I had made it that way. I had control. Now I had nothing.

I could feel it coming, swarming me from deep inside. That gnawing of your heart, like some little bug was devouring it before moving onto your lungs. You can't breathe. You can't do anything but sink as your chest caves in, and the despair, that fucking maddening sadness, eradicates every fiber of your being. I wasn't Dex Foray. I was just this emotion that was crumbling to the floor, holding onto the doorway like it was the last thread of my humanity.

I don't know how long I spent on the floor, crying tears that were too common to be embarrassed by, my heart continuously collapsing until I was nothing but that husk again. But when I did come to, I crawled to the kitchen, Fat Rabbit licking my face as if he had the power to make me smile, and grabbed a bottle of vodka out of the cupboard. It wasn't what I wanted, but at the moment, it was what I needed. I drank half of it before the darkness settled in my bones and there was oblivion and relief.

Unfortunately, you need to keep drinking if you want to stay unconscious. I woke up at about eight at night, Fat Rabbit clawing at the balcony door, wanting to be let out. I wiped my face on my shirt, my breath stinking like stale cigarettes, and got off the floor to let him out. It was colder than a nun's vagina outside, the low clouds glowing orange from the city lights and promising snow. The last time it snowed was when Perry left. I couldn't help but see the exquisite pain on her face as she ripped off that anchor bracelet and escaped into the snowy night, to places I was too afraid to go.

"God, I'm fucked," I said to the dog as he took a leak on the railing. He was judging my parenting skills again, I could tell. Well, let him. At the moment, he was eons more evolved than I was.

Call me a sap, or perhaps a dumb shit who loves torturing himself, but I needed to feel Perry's presence, to wallow in the way things were, to pretend. I needed it like I needed air, as if I would drown if I couldn't get it. Since stalking her was out of the question—I wasn't *that* guy—the next best thing was to retreat to the den, to the last place where she'd been.

The den was always my office, my sanctuary, the place that belonged to me—my man cave, if you will. It's funny, I had bought the apartment with my money (well, my mother's inheritance), and Jenn hadn't contributed a lick of anything, not even rent. Yet she'd wiped her skanky hands all over the place, as if it belonged more to her. But this room, no, this room had been mine, and for a very brief yet beautiful time, it had been Perry's too.

I sat on the single bed, breathing in air that no longer carried her scent, picturing Perry in there. First, I imagined her asleep in that little concert tee of hers, the hem exposing her sexy stomach, her breasts rising and falling with each breath, so perfectly contoured and ready for smothering—okay, maybe I *was* that guy. Then I imagined her rushing in, eyes brimming with tears, while I sat out on the couch, trying to figure out what I was going to do now that I was in love with my best friend, someone that didn't love me back. I saw her throwing her things in her bag, suffocating from my betrayal, my callousness, my cowardly fears.

I had to catch my breath again. The memory of it all pierced through me and pierced hard. My self-loathing ran as dangerously deep as my love for her. Perhaps the two were connected. I got up and flicked on my computer, setting my iTunes to shuffle. Depeche Mode's "Mercy In You" played and I pretended it didn't mean anything.

The video of our time in the mental asylum was still on my computer. After submitting it to Jimmy, I hadn't talked to him. Rebecca had been acting as mediator, shuffling messages between us. He knew I was alive and partnerless, I knew he wanted to talk. None of it meant anything anymore. I couldn't give a shit about Experiment in Terror. The experiment failed.

And then my eyes rested on the EVP recorder sitting beside the monitor, the earphones neatly folded underneath it. Perry had been the last person to listen to it.

"Please don't listen to it until tomorrow," she had said after having a weird reaction to it. "It makes no sense to me but I think it will to you."

I gingerly picked up the recorder and straightened out the headset. I hesitated before inserting it into my ears, then took a deep breath and went for it. What the hell had been on this tape? What was it that caused her to kiss my forehead and tell me I had nothing to worry about? Usually when someone pulls that line on you, you've got a fuckload of problems coming your way.

I swallowed hard and pressed play. Static came on and I

turned the volume up a bit. Nothing. I scanned back to a minute earlier and let it go.

A voice spoke that caused my balls to shrivel up.

"I'm being watched," Creepy Clown Lady's voice came on. "We all are. By the soulless ones who keep us here. The demons."

It was too close to my ears, to my brain. I pulled the earphones out a tad, as if that would prevent her from coming through, and scanned even further back. I went back to listening, hearing only footsteps echo. It must have been the hallway back at the asylum. Then, everything went completely dead, like the sound and life were sucked out of the recorder.

"Declan, Declan," her voice came back on. "Declan, can you hear me? You should hear me now. You should see me soon. Your medication no longer works. She switched it on you."

My head hurt. Creepy Clown Lady was talking to me. Telling me my what? My medication didn't work? She switched it? Who? Perry? That made no sense.

Clown Lady's voice continued. "It is for the best. You need to be yourself. That's the only way we connect again. You need to remember me. Remember your Pippa. I know it's hard, you don't want to remember the past. Neither of you do. But it's time to accept what happened. What happened to both of you. I wish my family had let me stay with you, Declan. You needed someone to take care of you. Someone who loved you like I did."

Fuck this.

I quickly hit stop and shoved the devil's machine away from me. Was I still fucking wasted or what? There was no way in hell, no way that I could be hearing what I thought I was hearing. My pulse quickened, the veins in my wrist throbbing as I tried to wrap my head around it.

I put the earphones back in and pressed play again. Creepy Clown Lady repeated herself, and this time her words were sinking in. Not only what she was saying, but how she was saying it. Her voice. Her accent. Pippa.

My Pippa.

I was flooded with memories—some horrible, some wonderful—all of them involving a woman that was more like my mother than my mother ever was. She had been old then too, but her spirit was balls out, so much so that I couldn't place her age. She didn't look like the ghostly apparition I had first seen on Bainbridge Island back in the summer. She didn't seem like anything that could have loved and cared for me the way that Pippa did.

She went on, as if knowing how confused and/or drunk I'd be. "Remember the days we used to spend down in Central Park? The ghosts that walked among us? I'm one of them now. But I'm different. Because I was different before. Just like you. I can cross over when I choose. But I have to be careful. I'm being watched, we all are. By the soulless ones who keep us here. The demons."

Suddenly the ring of a phone—my phone?—blasted across the earphones. On the tape, I answered the phone. Perry was no doubt on the other line.

The phone call didn't disturb Pippa in the slightest. "I don't suppose you will hear this until later since you don't seem to hear me now. But when you hear this, know that I'll be around if I can and when I can. It's getting trickier to see you. I'm being watched, as I said. So I need you to stop all your medication, Declan. It's time to face what you are. And what Perry is. And who I am to you. To both of you. Perry, if you're listening...ask your parents who Declan

O'Shea is. And watch them carefully. You'll get the truth that I am not allowed to reveal."

The recorder went back to static and fuzz. I slowly removed the earphones and sat back in my chair.

What. The. Shit?

The room swirled around me as my brain, my poor drunk and bruised brain, tried to sift through Pippa's message and find the meaning in it. It was too much. Way too fucking much.

My dead nanny was haunting me, and Perry too. Somehow Perry's parents knew my real name—but how and why? It was time for us to face what we were. But what was that? And I had to stop taking my medication.

My head reeled some more as I recalled what Pippa had said earlier on. Perry had switched my medication. That was why I had been seeing ghosts up until recently. That's why I'd seen Abby when I had never seen her before. Not since my breakdown anyway.

That had to be a mistake though. Perry would never, *ever* switch my meds on me. That wasn't her style. She was honest to a fault. Well, apart from the whole telling me she wasn't in love with me bit.

Oh god.

I jumped to my feet and brought my hollowed out book from the shelf. I took out my pills, the ones I had consistently been taking and really studied them. At first glance they seemed fine. But one of the bottles had a little bit more in it than the others did, which didn't make sense since I always had to take an equal amount of each.

I cleared my desk and shook out the contents in neat little piles and then slowly started going through them, counting each pill, looking for irregularities. The bottle that was the most full had sixteen more pills than the other ones did. That didn't bode well. I picked up one of the small yellow ones and peered at it—Z over 3926. I'd never examined my pills closely enough to know if it said that before, so I quickly hopped on Google.

In a second I learned that it was five milligrams of diazepam. Valium.

And yet, somehow I couldn't believe it. There had to be some weird mistake. Perry would never do that to me. She couldn't...she wouldn't.

I looked at the white pills next. There wasn't a mark on them; they were smooth and clean. But that didn't seem right either. Those were my anti-hallucinogens, the strongest you could get. They'd have to be marked. With panic reaching around me like one bad-ass boa constrictor, I Googled the name of my medication. It should have R20 0168 on it. Or 7655 or something.

These had nothing. They weren't my medication.

I'd been taking low-grade Valium and a mystery pill for the last few weeks. My other pills still seemed to be what they were, but that wasn't enough to keep me at an even keel.

Perry had switched my medication on me, for who knows what reason. She'd seen me freaking the fuck out in an alleyway, terrified out of my mind. She'd heard me tell her about the mental institute. She was there to hear it all, my soul laid bare in complete honesty. She watched me suffer, she discovered my deepest fears.

And she hadn't said anything.

For the first time in a while I was able to ignore the heartache—the extreme, gut-wrenching betrayal—as anger came buzzing through me like kamikaze pilots. I was mad. I was livid. I was enraged. Nothing else that happened, nothing that I'd heard on the tapes, meant anything to me at that moment. All I could see and feel was that Perry had fucked with my life like I was some god damn science experiment and lied through her brilliant teeth while she watched me succumb.

I welcomed the anger with clenched fists and open arms.

THREE

Apparently, the world didn't stop just because you did. Despite the days I spent in an emotional coma, drinking and smoking my way out of my web of lies, Christmas was still approaching. I didn't really notice unless I left the house, popping in at the shop across the street to get my jugs of beer-to-go and bottles of wine. The twinkling lights, Mariah Carey music, and false cheer were like the final nail in my coffin. Life was going on at its shitastic rate, and yet, there I was, smelly, barely clothed, and drinking myself to death. It didn't fit. No one deserved to feel better than I did. I wanted everyone to know the endless rage and sorrow that wouldn't scrub away. It wasn't fair that they escaped and I didn't.

Sometimes I really hated Perry. I'd think about her and feel nothing but this animosity, this dark fuel that filtered through my veins like sludge. I wallowed in it, embracing the hate, dancing with it, for hate was a much more potent and powerful lover than sadness ever was. It made me feel vindicated and alive.

But in the mornings, it would fade. Over time, the anger

would subside. And so would the heartache. I was down to feeling nothing at all. It was brilliant.

Since I'd stopped caring, it made everything else easier to deal with. I still managed to take Fat Rabbit out for his walks, but other than that, I just didn't give a shit. I thought I was pretty good at it too. Once again, I was ignoring my phone calls. In fact, I forgot to charge my phone and left it dead. I didn't check emails. I didn't do anything.

Occasionally, I would think about Pippa's message to me. I guess I took some of it to my cold, cold heart, because I stopped taking my medication. If the ghosts came after me, so what? Who cared? It's not like I needed to better myself anymore. Besides, it might be fun to associate with the dead. They were the only ones who were as unfeeling and empty as I was. They'd be the perfect companions.

Then there was the whole thing about Declan O'Shea, which of course was my name until my mother died and I took her last name, Foray, to remember her by. Or at least remember my guilt. I finally came to the conclusion that if Perry's parents knew who I was, it probably had something to do with the Swedish Spectre of Clown College. Logic pointed to Pippa being Perry's grandmother or relative of some kind. But you know what? Whoop dee fucking do.

Yes, the no fucks to give stage was wonderful. I drank some more and ate tons of crap just because I could. I was sleepwalking through life, and that was good enough for me.

Unfortunately, it wasn't good enough for everyone. Apparently, I had friends and people who worried about me. I couldn't keep them out of my bubble for long.

It was two nights before Christmas when Rebecca and her girlfriend Emily showed up at my apartment. It took that moment for me to, once again, realize how out of control my life had gotten. I thought I was just fine, sitting on the balcony in the freezing cold, drinking my bourbon. I'd eaten bag after bag of Doritos and was feeling a little hot. That might account for why I was out there in my underwear. I mean, it all made valid sense in my head at the time. You're hot? Take off your clothes and sit outside in near freezing temperatures. Enjoy the view. Enjoy the darkness.

I don't remember all that much, except for the horror on their faces as I was shoved into the shower. Not a nice steamy shower to get my cold bones back to a normal state, but a cold shower that felt like murder on my frozen skin. So much for not feeling anything. I hollered and yelped as Rebecca practically assaulted me with cleaning products. Then I was even more helpless as she dried me off and put jeans and a thick sweater on me. Meanwhile, her partner in crime was out in the kitchen, pouring out every bottle of booze I had and throwing every bag of chips into the garbage.

Oh no, Hulk alert. Not my chips!

"Dex," Rebecca said, leading me toward the bedroom. "Pack your bags. We're taking you with us."

I glared at her as the waves of anger came back. Perry's betrayal, her hand squeezing my heart, it all came back in an ambush. Everything I was avoiding was still there.

I was too irate and overwhelmed to speak so Rebecca passed me off to Em, who kept her tiny hand affixed around my arm while Rebecca started packing for me.

"I know you don't want us to be here," she said, cramming my clothes into a small suitcase she dragged out from the closet. "I know you want to be left alone so you can continue drinking yourself into a selfish stupor like the arse that you are. But you don't have a choice. You're coming with us. We'll take care of you until you're back on your feet. I'm not saying you have to change who you are, but

Dex, you, right now, this is not you. You've given up. And the Dex Foray that I know, never gives up, no matter what life throws at him."

"Perry," I whispered, trying to find one leg to stand on. "She switched my medication and never told me. She wanted me to see the ghosts. She did that to me."

Rebecca paused and gave me a thoughtful look. "And you have every right to be angry. So be angry, Dex. It's better than being nothing at all."

I felt like I was choking. My words came out hoarsely as I gasped for air, as I allowed myself to feel. "It hurts more than I know what to do with. I can't handle this. I can't."

Em squeezed my arm lightly and started stroking my back. Rebecca sighed and came over to me, placing her hands on either side of my face. "You're one of my dearest friends," she told me, tilting my head down so she could look me square in the eye. "I have a pretty good idea of what you can handle. You'll get over this, Dex. Perry will too. Whether that means you'll be back in each other's lives, if that's even what you'd both want, I don't know. But she hurt you. And you hurt her. Even though you're apart, you're in this together. You'll get out of it together."

She gave my cheek a light slap. "So buck up. Put on your big boy knickers and deal with it like everyone else has to when they get their heart broken. People lie and they hurt you and they betray you. But they also make mistakes. You haven't been the perfect guy with her, Dex. Apart from the way things ended, she had to be only your friend the whole time you were with Jenn. She had to love you and suffer because you were too scared to move on and make her yours. Does it make you feel better to know that she was probably dying slowly inside, that you were breaking her heart bit by bit?"

I swallowed hard. I felt better—for one second. Then it passed, my anger going with it.

"No," I admitted softly. "It doesn't."

Because even after all of this, I still loved her. Love and hate were two sides of the same coin, and my coin was destined to land with love facing up. And the minute I made peace with those odds was the minute I'd start winning.

"Come on." Em gave me a little tug. "You're in our hands now. You'll be back to your obnoxious old self in no time."

I was looking forward to it. My old self didn't have permanently orange-stained palms from an excessive Doritos consumption.

Originally, Emily and Rebecca thought they'd just show up at my place (I'd given my extra key to Rebecca now that Jenn was out of the picture) and drag me out to a holiday party. Once they saw my trailer trash state of affairs, however, their plans changed. I did go and live with them for about a week, and it was the best thing that could have happened to me. After falling one too many times, both of them made sure I was up again and that I stayed up.

That was the ball-sucking thing about heartache. It didn't follow logic or physics or any sort of rules. It wasn't that you started off in absolute grief and then slowly got better. It was a rollercoaster of emotions, from hate to love and back again. Each day was different. It was a roll of the dice, a turn of the cards.

Some days I'd feel fine. I had started eating better thanks to the girls and their new vegan lifestyle. Unfortunately, because I was spending Christmas with them now, it meant eating something called Tofurkey. Still, my body and mind were responding to the weird tasteless veggie loaf, rejoicing that I was filling up on healthy foods, and I felt like I could handle anything life threw at me.

But on other days, when I'd see a girl with a fantastic, excessive ass, or hear Slayer on the radio, I was plunged into turmoil. I'd be reminded of Perry, of what she was to me, and I wished I could have realized how I felt sooner. I wished I could have told her how I really felt, that she was more than a friend and a partner, that she was my everything. The only person who really understood—who really loved me for me. But if wishes were fishes, this whole place would really stink.

A few days after New Year's, when I was back at my apartment with Fat Rabbit, trying to piece my life back together, I got a call from my friend Dean. Dean was a good guy, dependable and funny, and the co-host of Gamers with our friend Seb. I guessed that even though Dean had a good physique and slim build, he'd yielded to one too many video games lately and was looking to get back in shape. I had a feeling that Rebecca had probably let him know that I'd devolved from a dick-grabbing monkey to a defecating parasite (which, by the way, is much worse), and I needed help.

Dean had the goal of entering a few half-marathons and wanted me to train with him. He said he needed the motivation and accountability and that I was the perfect match. Now, don't get me wrong, I'm no stranger to a little exercise. But knowing Dean, our training sessions would start making up half of our lives. It was a good thing then that I didn't have a life anymore.

The first couple of weeks were the toughest, but fuck did it feel good to put my body through the ringer rather than my heart. When we were running I didn't have energy to think. All I could do was put one foot in front of the other, pushing through the pain in my shins or my lungs that were threatening to explode. It was cathartic and torturous at the same time. Hurt so good.

Then we started weight training. Dean was African American so it was extremely unfair that he bulked up in what seemed like days, whereas for me it was a slower process. But with my diet improving (I tried to follow Rebecca's diet, except that I was back to eating meat...worst vegan ever) and my alcohol intake cut drastically, I could see the changes. And as my body improved, my mind improved. My soul improved. Everything was feeling stronger.

The great thing about Dean was that we never talked about anything too serious. He never asked me about my family or my past or ghosts or Perry. All talk about women was carefree and easy and he let me be the pervert that I was.

But I guess on one suspiciously sunny day, his curiosity had gotten the better of him. While we were winding down our run at Lawton Park, he said, "So, Perry. Were you in love with her?"

I nearly tripped over my own feet and caught myself before I face-planted into a tree. "What the hell kind of question is that?" I asked, fighting for my breath.

He shrugged, which is kind of hard to do when you're running.

"It's a good question," he said with a sly smile. "Everyone wants to know what made Dex Foray fall to his knees."

"Oh, is that so?"

"What can I say, man? You're a celebrity at Shownet.

People care about what happens to you. Besides, Jimmy told everyone you went crazy and tried to eat your dog or something so he had to put you on sabbatical. I figure if you tried to eat that fat thing, someone must have broken your heart good."

I slowed down my pace, finding it difficult to defend myself and exercise at the same time.

"I didn't try to eat my dog...and I'm not on sabbatical. I haven't even talked to Jimmy since all this shit happened."

"Dude, you know when you pull that shit, you're on sabbatical. No one can just leave Shownet, especially not Mr. Popular like you. Well, actually it was Perry that was Mrs. Popular. So tell me, were you in love with her? What happened?"

I don't know why I thought it was anyone's business to know that, but with the whole turning over a new leaf and becoming a new man thing, I figured being honest would be a good start. Lying had never done me any good before.

I exhaled hard and chewed on my lip for a few beats. "Yes. I was in love with her. And to be honest with you, homeboy, I still am."

"Shit, Dex. First you say you're in love with her, then you call me homeboy? Who the hell are you?"

I rolled my eyes as we jogged through a grove of Douglas firs. "Why does everyone act so surprised when I admit that? I'm not the motherfucking Tin Man. I have a heart."

"Apparently. So what happened?"

"Didn't Rebecca tell you?" I asked wryly.

He shook his head. "No. You and Perry were totally humping each other with your eyes at the Christmas party though, so it was kind of obvious that something was going to happen."

"Well I guess you could say we took eye humping to the next level. Then I freaked the fuck out because I realized I was in love with her, and she had told me earlier that she wasn't in love with me."

"Whoa, wait up," Dean said, slowing down to a fast walk. "She told you she wasn't in love with you? Before you had sex with her? How the hell did that come up?"

Good question. Because I was an idiot and had to ask, that's why.

I told him as much.

"Okay, man, seriously," he said, holding up his hand, palm out. "You mean to tell me that you asked her, point blank, whether she loved you or not. Before you even had a clue that you loved her. And you believed her when she said she didn't?"

"Uh, yeah. I trusted her."

"You don't know shit about women, do you?" Dean actually sounded a bit angry.

I frowned. "I know how to get them off."

"Not good enough, my man. Put yourself in her fine shoes for a moment. She's in love with you—that was quite obvious from what I saw, but I can see you're a bit of a dumbass about the whole thing. So she's in love with you and suddenly you ask her if she loves you. You don't say, 'oh babe I love you' or any shit like that to give her an idea of where it's going. You just ask her, like you're being good ol' fuck-with-you Foray. Of course she's going to lie! What would her alternative have been? To tell the truth and have you laugh at her or act all smug on some ego trip?"

"Hey," I sniped, "I wouldn't have done any of that. I would have told her how I felt."

He jammed his finger in my face. "Only after she had to go first. What were you trying to do, test her? That's not cool, man, not cool. You would have lied if you were in her shoes, that's what I'm saying."

"Are you trying to make me feel bad?" I asked. My lungs and heart couldn't handle the revelation. I stopped, leaning against a tree, feeling hotter by the second as the sweat streamed off me.

"No, man," Dean said, stopping beside me. "I'm trying to tell you you're an idiot for freaking the fuck out, that's what."

"Thanks."

"So then what happened? You kicked her out of bed or what?"

I rubbed my sweaty palms on my face. "Pretty much. Then I figured out the whole thing that you had no problem picking up on. And then it was too late."

"I got to tell you, that sucks," he said. "And you're an idiot."

Majorly. I was overheating now, feeling trapped in my shirt. So much for turning over a new leaf. The rollercoaster was heading down again.

Dean shook his head in mild pity and started stretching. I took off my shirt, trying to get some cold air on my skin, vaguely aware that with the way Dean and I were posed, him bending over and me sweaty and shirtless, we could have been in a gladiator porn. I suppose that was an option if I wanted to come back to Shownet.

It didn't help that he was staring at my chest.

"What? Am I giving you a hard-on?" I asked.

He shook his head and gave me a nasty look. "No, I'm reading your tattoo. And with madness comes the light."

"I got it a long time ago. To remind me."

"Remind you of what?"

"That madness isn't all bad."

A chilly breeze picked up and I slid my soaked t-shirt back on, shivering from the contact.

"Ain't all bad?" he said. "Madness is not your friend, Dex. You just treat it like one."

"I didn't say it was my friend," I said quietly, feeling a bit weird discussing it with someone. I never even talked about it with Jenn. "I'm saying I made the most of it. Sometimes you have to fall pretty fucking far before you can see the light. Believe me, I've been through some shit that I wouldn't wish on my worst enemy."

Dean's face grew serious. "I believe you. So, what's the light then? What makes the madness worth it?"

Shit. Dean and I had gone from workout buddies to acting like a bunch of overanalyzing pussies. Next thing you knew, we'd start having our periods at the same time.

Yet, pussy or not, I kept talking. "Perry was my light. I didn't know it at the time, but I know it now. And in her light, I lost that madness. It only came back when she left." I paused, looking around at the tall trees and the sun streaming through them, unable to stop my mouth from going on. "She makes me want to live life as it should be lived. By the balls, you know."

"Makes," he mused, stretching his hamstring.

"Makes?"

"Yeah man. Makes. Present tense. She *makes* you want to be a better man. She's still your light, no matter what the rest of this shit is. That's pretty deep."

"Balls deep?" I asked.

"Dude, enough with your balls. Maybe that should be your next tattoo."

I raised one brow. "Balls deep. I guess it would be applicable to the ladies."

He sighed impatiently. "No. Perry is your light. She

helped you lose the madness. Something like that. To balance out the other one."

"Dedicate a tattoo to her?" I asked.

He shrugged. "You're still in love with her. She makes you want to live life. Personally, and this is just me, man, if I ever met a woman who saved me that way, I'd devote some temples to her or something. That's how the Taj Mahal got started, I'm sure."

We hadn't even left the park before a phrase started floating around in my head—*Within your light, I lose the madness.*

FOUR

Even though my man Dean had been the one to give me the tattoo idea, I decided to take Rebecca along to accompany me during the procedure. It's funny that I already had two tattoos and this one would also be simple cursive behind my shoulder, yet needles kind of freaked me out. I didn't like to admit it, but hey, the whole becoming a new man thing had me spewing a lot of shit I used to keep to myself. Which was just what the world needed—an even more uncensored Dex Foray.

I didn't know if I was just on a down day or if I was jonesing because I'd just quit smoking, but I was a pile of nerves as the tattoo artist did his work on me.

Rebecca noticed. "Does it hurt?" she asked as the first few words were completed.

I shook my head. It didn't. Didn't mean it was comfortable and it didn't mean I liked it, but it definitely didn't hurt.

She pursed her lips and looked me over inquisitively. "Do you mind if I get Perry's address off of you?"

I flinched. Luckily the artist was fast enough to feel it coming and lifted the needle away just in time.

"What?" I asked.

"Are we okay?" said the tattoo artist.

I nodded quickly at him and the machine resumed its buzzing.

I lowered my voice. "Why do you want her address?"

"It's not like that," she said, taking a tube out of her bag that probably used to be a hamster and dotting sticky gloss on her lips. "Em and I might be in Portland soon and I was thinking—"

"Don't you dare," I warned her. "Don't you dare go see her."

She lowered her brows and snapped her purse shut with a deafening click. "Dex, please. She was my friend, too."

"I'm your friend first."

"*You're* not going to go see her."

"Obviously not, she hates my guts."

"But you're getting a tattoo because of her."

"Well I'm not dragging the tattoo artist over there and getting it inked on her forehead, am I?"

"I just want to see how she's doing. I'm worried about her."

I wished she hadn't said that, because I was worried as hell about her, too. Over the last week, I'd thought about Pippa's message again and again, trying to figure out what it all meant. Why it was a warning. How Perry was doing. Just because I'd been mercifully free from seeing ghosts—despite no medication—it didn't mean Perry was. I couldn't imagine how she'd deal with it all alone. Even though, looking back, I hadn't been much help—partially because of the medication, partially because I was afraid—I knew she had felt safer with me. Because I always believed her and I understood. Now who knew what was going on? I had little faith in her younger sister, Ada, and zero faith in her parents.

"Fine," I said. "But I didn't send you."

"I know you didn't. And I know you want to know how she is. I just want to make sure she's fine and see if I can help in any way if she's not."

I nodded and gave her a stern look. "Watch out for her mom. She bites."

Half an hour later, the tattoo was complete. I felt lighter already.

A FEW DAYS LATER I HEARD BACK FROM REBECCA. SHE went to Perry's and things hadn't exactly gone as planned. I was torn between wanting as much information from her as possible and trying to protect my heart. In the end, my stupid, self-destructive tendencies demanded every single detail from her. I'd really lost it. That guy who wasn't about to stalk her? Well I felt like I was mentally stalking her as I made Rebecca describe what she looked like. She sounded as beautiful as ever, darkness and light all wrapped up into one. My heart twisted itself into a well-worn knot.

"She looked tired though," she told me over the phone while I got ready to go to the corner store. I was having Dean and Seb over for some drinks before we hit up the bars, something I hadn't done in an extremely long time.

"What kind of tired?" I asked. Perry had fair skin that usually rebelled when she didn't get enough sleep. Yeah, yeah, I'm a creeper who noticed those things. I didn't say she still wasn't gorgeous when she was tired. It made her look more vulnerable than ever, and that, combined with her delicious tits that were just ripe for squeezing were a fucking lethal combination.

"I don't know," she said. "I caught her coming back from a run, so maybe it was just that. Or perhaps it was the fact that she wanted to throw my arse to the curb. It was hard to tell."

Regardless, I made her tell me everything all over again, going over every word she said. Perhaps, if Rebecca repeated it enough, it would be like talking to Perry herself.

It wasn't, but in some sick way, it was close. Hearing this gave me a sense of closure that I didn't have before, relief that she, as tired as she might have been, was okay. She was alive and out there in the world, living her life, working a new job. She'd moved on, and as much as that stung the shit out of me worse than any wasp could, I was somewhat happy for her.

Of course, being happy for her made me feel more miserable for me. Call me a selfish dickmonkey, but it's hard to be happy for someone when you can't share their happiness with them. I wanted to be there with her as she lived her life, watching for those rare smiles on her face.

I was grumbling about that to myself as I pulled my coat around me and braved the cold, crossing underneath the monorail tracks to the store. I tied Fat Rabbit outside and went inside, searching the aisle for the cheapest bottle of wine. I was unemployed now and wasn't about to waste a drop of expensive shit on Dean and Seb, not when they'd probably be puking it up later anyway.

It was just a small convenience store, and while the douchester hipbag guy behind the counter—Paul I think his name was—dealt with a customer at the jugs of beer-to-go (who knew it would be so popular?), I waited at the register, watching a lady with interest.

I'd seen her a few times before…in fact, lately I think she'd been in the store every time I was there. She wore all black, with a furry velvet hat that looked vaguely Russian. I'd never seen her face; she would just walk from the counter, down the aisle to the end, like she was part zombie. You know the way really old people walk when they're too stubborn for scooters or a cane? That kind of walk. Slow, deliberate, and shaking slightly. I'd never seen her look at anything on the shelves or buy anything. She just did that ultra-slow walk of hers.

"Ready to go?" Douchester Hipbag said to me. I straightened up off the counter and pushed the bottle of wine toward him.

"Sure am."

"Still not smoking?" he asked as he rang it up.

"Still not," I told him and turned my attention back to the woman. I nodded in her direction. "Hey, what's the deal with the Walking Dead reject over there?"

He frowned and looked past me. "What do you mean?"

"I mean," I said, watching her do her death dance. "What's her deal? I always see her here, just…acting like a zombie."

Paul gave me a funny look and popped the wine into a paper bag. "I don't know who you're talking about, Dex."

I looked at the lady and back at him. "Uh, you can't see that lady there?"

He shook his head. "I think quitting smoking might have done something to your brain."

It wasn't quitting smoking that did something to my brain. Oh fucknuts. There was no lady, was there?

I quickly handed him the five dollars and snatched my

wine up off the counter. I eyed her form differently now, the jerky way her limbs moved, the fact that I always saw her in the same place, doing the same actions. She wasn't a zombie, but she was in fact dead.

I got myself out of the store, feeling the heebie jeebies crawling up and down my skin, and Fat Rabbit and I practically ran across the road to my apartment. Even though the lady wasn't a threat (not yet anyway), I was scared shitless. I wasn't used to seeing them alone, and I suddenly needed Perry's embrace and comfort more than anything in the world.

Fortunately, it didn't take long for Dean and Seb to show up. Unfortunately, I'd drunk the bottle of wine already. They never even had a chance.

"You're getting a nice head start, aren't you?" Dean said as he placed a six-pack of beer in the fridge. I guess he figured he'd need to bring his own.

"Well, I just saw a ghost, so I'm feeling a bit...uh, on edge."

Seb and Dean exchanged a look. Dean frowned, his eyes cautious underneath his glasses. Seb just laughed and tucked his long hair behind his ears.

"Awesome," he said, cracking open a beer. "You saw a ghost, that's rad."

Seb was always kind of a stoner. Swap kind of for totally. I had a feeling he was a cast member on *That '70s Show* at one point but he got fired or something and now just lived his life stuck in that world. I mean, it's an off the wall theory, but I see ghosts, so what the fuck do I know?

"Yeah, Seb. A ghost. And it's not awesome. It's scary as shit."

"Right on."

I shook my head and wished I had more wine. "Beer

me," I said, holding out my hand. Dean sighed and tore a beer off the rings, handing it to me.

They pulled up the barstools and we tried to talk about a chick, Clarissa, that Seb was attempting to bang, but the conversation kept coming back to ghosts. As if ghosts were more interesting than sex. *Nothing* was more interesting than sex.

"So, like, I totally thought Perry was like ghost whisperer," Seb said, rocking back and forth on the stool, "and you were just the camera guy. I didn't know you saw ghosts too, dude."

I twisted the metal ring around and round until it snapped off the can.

"Normally I don't. I'm…" I shot them both a quick glance. They were watching me intently. "I'm off my medication. I was put away in a mental institute back in college because I saw ghosts. They thought I was crazy. They put me on meds—robbing me of my real life while they were at it—and I stopped seeing them. I haven't taken any pills since December."

Both of them grew silent. Seb looked confused and Dean's face hadn't changed. He still watched me carefully, judging my sanity, or if perhaps I was a big fat liar. I didn't blame him. I hoped he'd still be my running buddy, but if he wanted to hang out with saner people, I definitely wasn't the right fit for him.

"But you're not crazy," Seb offered slowly, as if reading my mind. "Just because you see ghosts doesn't mean you're crazy."

I shot him a smile. "Doesn't it? That's never what the doctors said."

He took a long yet thoughtful sip of his beer. "I think doctors don't know shit. I bet if you see ghosts, it's not because you're mental. You're just different, Dex. And that's okay."

This was getting borderline heartwarming. Must put a stop to it.

"Anyway, that's neither here nor there," I said, raising my beer in the air. "Forget ghosts, let's say thanks for sex and get Seb here laid tonight."

We rammed our beer cans together, foam spilling over the sides.

"Just Seb?" Dean asked, wiping beer off his can.

"I thought you and your new lady friend were exclusive," I told him.

"Naw, we are. I meant you. You're not getting any tail?"

I snorted at his choice of words. "Tail. No, I'm not."

Seb slammed his drink down and wiped his mouth. "Why not? Dude, you're single. Maybe Clarissa has a hot sister or something. Or maybe one of the bartenders she works with will dig you."

"I really hope you're talking about female bartenders, Sea Bass," I warned him. "I know I've been spending a lot of time sweating with Dean here, but..."

"So that's it?" Dean asked. "You're just going to spend your life pining after her?"

I narrowed my eyes. "Dean, if I'm not mistaken, you're the one who said I should build a temple for her or something."

"That was then. I thought maybe you'd have gone after her. Isn't this why you're...what was it again...becoming a better man?"

It was. But just because I wasn't going to her now, didn't mean it was off the table.

"When was the last time you got laid?" Seb asked.

I didn't have to think. I'd been jerking off to it ever since. "With Perry. After the Christmas party."

His jaw dropped. "Oh man, you so need to get some action tonight. Hell, you can have Clarissa if you want."

"Oh, like you're doing me a favor by passing up the chick you haven't even fucked yet."

"Fine. Offer is off the table now. Your loss."

"I don't need anyone's help getting laid. I never have." I didn't mean to brag but...okay, yes, I totally meant to brag. I pulled back the sleeve of my t-shirt. "And look at these guns." I eyed Dean. "Don't you dare show off yours, cuz that's not fair. But seriously, with these guns and my face and my dick, women are completely powerless."

Dean sat back and crossed his arms. "Maybe not all women."

"Perry hasn't been invited to the brand new gun show yet," I told him, as if there was a chance in hell that she'd see me now. "When she does, all will be forgiven."

"I see," Dean mused. "So, before that happens, whenever that happens, are you going to get busy with some fine ladies tonight or keep sitting here talking about your guns?"

I pushed back my stool and stood up. "That sounds like a challenge."

"As your running coach, it's my job to challenge you."

"Hey now, we're *running* partners."

"You guys sound really gay," Seb spoke up.

We both glared at him in unison. He threw up his hands. "What, I'm not judging. I'd be happy if you were gay —I'd get more action that way."

I rolled my eyes and pointed my beer at Dean. "You want me to get some tonight? Challenge accepted."

He grinned in response before chugging the rest of his beer.

Seb looked between us with a dumb smile on his face. "So are you getting some men or women tonight, Dex?"

This was going to be a long night.

~

A FEW HOURS LATER, WE ENDED UP DRUNK AS SKUNKS at this really divey metal bar called The Funhouse. The band playing was loud as fuck, pure metal, and the bartender was Clarissa, the fairly hot chick that Seb was pining over. I say fairly hot since black lipstick and bleached hair wasn't really my thing, but he seemed to be head over heels for her. Clarissa, on the other hand, had a range of suitors to deal with, all hanging around the bar.

We ended up doing the same for a bit, hiding from the noise of the venue's shitty PA system. While Clarissa didn't have a sister or a bartending buddy, she did have some friends who were there to see the terrible band. Seb was doing his best to get in good with them so he could then score in good with her. Men were so fucking predictable. The women ate it up though, as Seb played his harmless stoner card. I suppose all you had to do was wear a puppy dog face and women would do anything to help you.

Well, it didn't work that way with me. I never had to work very hard for women, which was both a blessing and a curse. Mainly a blessing, since I never complained about having too many chicks to fuck. Still, I did feel a bit off balance as I watched Seb do his thing. I had been with Jenn for so long that I'd forgotten what it was like to be single again. With Perry, everything was easy and effortless. It wasn't a matter of a girl wanting to suck my dick, but a matter of me wanting to suck hers. I mean, her proverbial one. Man, Seb had done a number on me.

There hadn't been anyone in the bar who remotely caught my eye until I went to the ATM to get more money out. The damn machine was taking forever and had the nerve to charge me a four dollar transaction fee. I was ready to throttle the thing until I turned around and saw an interesting face looking back at me.

She was tall, maybe my height (damn my height!), with long, wavy red hair and matching lipstick. Her eyes were glazed like she'd just been fucked and fucked good, and her lips were held in a half snarl, as if she was about to blow cigarette smoke in my face.

"Sorry," I apologized. I didn't know why I apologized since I hadn't run into her or anything, but then I found my eyes focusing on her amazing rack that pulled her thin white tank top tight across her chest. Her nipples had made themselves known, speaking to me, whispering "bite me."

I rarely got caught with my eyes where they shouldn't be so I quickly averted my eyes back to hers. It was hard to tell in the bar, but they could have been a dark blue. They were nasty looking, like she was going to eat me alive and enjoy every crunch. I liked that.

I liked it a lot. I had a boner in two second flat and was hard as fuck, straining against my pants. Part of me wanted to feel embarrassed, the other part wanted to rub it up and down on her while I rejoiced that I had finally gotten a hard-on over someone other than Perry. I finally found a woman's proverbial dick to suck.

I needed a better saying.

"Are you with the band?" the woman asked in a low, husky voice. The hairs on the back of my neck stood up. She had a nice pink tongue that probably matched the rest of her nice pink bits.

I smirked at her. "These fucks? No."

She smiled back, totally bitchy, totally hot. "Well, I am. I guess I'm one of these fucks, too."

Oh mama. I loved the way her lips looked when she said fuck. I loved the way her eyes looked when she said it, too. She wanted some of this, and judging by the heat I was packing in my pants, I couldn't blame her.

"What were you saying about fucking?" I asked, taking a step toward her. I wasn't normally so forward, but I obviously didn't have any blood left in my head.

She grinned and touched my shirt. "I asked because you have an eyebrow ring and a shirt that looks like it used to fit you in the '90s. I didn't say anything about fucking, but now that the card is on the table, maybe you can prove to be more manly than you look."

I grinned right back at her, my eyes drifting over her shoulder and toward the bathroom door. Nailing someone in the bathroom of a grungy metal bar was probably one of the grossest, dirtiest things you could do. But I felt like bathing in dirt after being so clean for the last month.

"Can I buy you a drink?" I asked her, remembering my manners before I got carried away.

She put her hand on my chest and slid it down until it reached the waistband of my boxer briefs. I don't know why I was worried about being dirty when I'd only last a couple of minutes, tops.

"I'm good," she said slowly. "But you go get yourself one. I'll just be in the women's washroom, right over there."

Message was received loud and clear. I watched her sashay her tight little jean-clad ass over to the washroom and disappear inside. I had maybe two minutes before I would join her and suddenly I was nervous as fuck.

I went over to the bar and got Clarissa's attention long enough to order a shot of bourbon. After I put it back and tried to gather up my courage, which had somehow disappeared along with the blood in my brain, Dean appeared beside me.

"Saw you talking to that hot piece of ass," he commented, leaning forward on his elbows.

"I guess you could call it talking," I said, wishing I had another shot. I raised my hand for Clarissa and waited. "It was more like 'let's fuck,' but not said as vaguely as that."

"You know, I always thought you had a type," he mused.

"What do you mean?" I asked as Clarissa filled up my shot glass again and down the hatch it went. What the hell was wrong with me? Even my erection was deflating, like I was losing all my nerve, like I was all talk and no show.

"Oh, the bitchy look. Like Jenn, like the redhead. Gorgeous and all that, but mean. You know, you can tell when a girl ain't got no heart. And you like that. That's why I was so surprised that you fell in love with Perry."

I fell in love with Perry. I was in love with Perry.

"She was so sweet and cute and somewhat innocent. Not the girl who would screw you in a shithole. Not a girl who would ever hurt you on purpose. You know, she was nice. And well, you don't like nice, Dex. You like bitches. You like to be treated like shit for some god damn reason, and I don't know why. You don't deserve it. But maybe you think you do."

"Dean," I said slowly, pushing my shot glass away from me. "Have you been listening to a lot of self-help tapes lately?"

"I'm just saying, man. It's interesting. I feel like I'm finally cracking the Foray code."

Time was ticking away. The redhead was still in the bathroom, probably waiting for the last chick to leave so she could barricade the door, avoiding the puddles of vomit and piss in her platform shoes. Was that really what I wanted? Now that I was called to act upon it, my dick argued against it. It didn't give a fuck and I meant that literally. I wanted the easy bitch because it was safe and familiar. And let's face it, I was horny as hell.

But that wasn't me anymore. I'd seen the light. I wanted the girl who embodied it. I wanted to deserve her, to be the man she needed. And I'd do whatever I could to be that man.

I sighed and slapped a few bills on the table. I smacked Dean on the arm. "I'm going home, buddy."

I pushed past him, waving at Seb as I went, who was still stuck in a conversation with one of Clarissa's friends.

"Does that mean I can have her?" Dean called out jovially from behind me.

"She's probably still in there," I answered back and walked out into the cold night. I was going home alone, and for the first time in a long time, that was completely okay with me. I, too, had a code to crack.

FIVE

With my life wrapped up in running, working out, and making myself extremely fuckable in Perry's eyes, a couple of weeks had flown by before I saw Rebecca again. She finally flagged me down and invited me out for pizza. I hated to be one of those guys who turned his nose up at the Italian pie, so I dragged my ass out the door, promising myself I'd do an extra session at the gym afterward.

"Dex, over here!"

I scanned the restaurant looking for the source of the smooth English accent that called my name. I swear, Rebecca's voice was on par with Morgan Freeman's in the voices I'd like to narrate my life category.

I saw her in the corner of the room and made my way over. The restaurant was a hipster-ish pizza joint not too far from my apartment and at 6:00 p.m. it was absolutely bustling. She looked delicious as usual, dressed from head to toe in a form-fitting black dress that gripped her hips and set off her vampire-pale skin.

She got out of her chair and went for a hug, her smile wider than normal. She wrapped her arms around me for a few tight seconds, then she stepped out of the embrace and placed her soft fingers around my bicep and gave another, heartier squeeze.

"So you've been sticking to it," she remarked, looking proud. "Good for you. You look fantastic."

I felt fantastic. Okay, that was bullshit. But I felt better than I had in weeks.

"You look gorgeous," I told her honestly and sat down at our cozy booth.

She gave me a coy wave, simultaneously brushing off the compliment and reveling in it as only she knew how, and ordered herself a drink when the waiter came by. I ordered a Jack and Coke, naturally.

She waited for the waiter to leave before she looked at me, surprised. "Really?"

I leaned back against the soft leather seat. "What?"

"I thought you were turning over a new leaf."

I snorted. "I have. I'm going to the gym every day, running, I quit smoking, I quit my meds. I can't give up all my vices. I'm not a superhero."

She twisted her cherry red lips around. She knew old habits died hard and was probably thinking back to Christmas when she and Em had to come rescue me. Man, that felt like ages ago.

"That's...all done with," I added, feeling defensive. "You know I was in a bad place at that time."

She smiled sadly and gave me a slow nod. "I know. I'm not judging. Frankly, I don't think I could hang out with you if you weren't the vice type of guy."

"Well then, you'll be pleased to know that I'm still drinking and I'm still wanking to porn."

"That's my boy," she said appraisingly. The waiter came back with our drinks and we said cheers over it.

"To friends," she said.

"To friends," I agreed.

I took a big slug of my drink, the bubbles fizzing my nose, causing me to tense up. With watering eyes I looked at Rebecca. She was staring at my arms with an odd look on her face.

"What?" I asked.

She shrugged. "I don't know, Dex, your arms, your shoulders…you look really good. It's nice to see."

"Good enough to make you switch sides?" I joked.

She took a sly sip of her drink. I had missed the harmless flirting with her. I'd missed her in general. Hanging out with her, Dean, and Seb made me realize how badly I'd neglected my friends when I was with Jenn. It sounded cliché as fuck and I hated that I'd actually missed out on this earlier.

"Well you better not tell Em then," I continued. "Actually, maybe you should tell her. See if she wants to get in on the Dex action, too." I winked at her.

She giggled. "Oh, you. Once a pig, always a pig. At least that hasn't changed."

I gave her a forced smile even though what she said stabbed at me a bit. That was the thing with Rebecca. She still felt some kinship with Perry, the very thing I still felt, and the fact that we were both to blame for our relationship's destruction was always on the surface.

Her face fell, which meant I wasn't doing a very good job of keeping my emotions under wraps. It was harder now when I was off the medication. I felt everything tenfold, and it was impossible to ignore at times. I felt sorry for women for having to deal with this emotional shit most of their lives.

I cleared my throat and anxiously picked up the menu,

absently looking for something to eat. Going off the meds also made me hungry—too hungry—another reason why working out was so important now.

"So how is Jenn?" I asked innocently. I didn't really want to know but I'd asked anyway. Seriously, I should get points for this. I hadn't asked about her since the breakup.

So, understandably, Rebecca looked a bit shocked. She lowered her voice and leaned in slightly. "Do you want me to tell you what you want to hear or do you want the truth?"

I shot her a quick glance, trying to play it cool. "It doesn't matter, I don't really care."

"She's doing well then. I'm not too happy about it, but it makes working with her easier."

I sucked in my breath and nodded. "Oh, yeah?"

Fuck Jenn. Why did I even ask that? Wait, I didn't care.

"Yeah," she continued, watching me carefully for some sort of meltdown. "I guess Bradley makes her happy. It's a weird sight to see. She's still an annoying cunt though."

I humored her choice of words with a smile and went back to trying to pick out a pizza. I *was* grateful that Jenn was out of my life, but it still hurt to hear what Rebecca was saying. I didn't miss Jenn, but I didn't think it was fair that she was happy after everything she'd done.

Rebecca reached over and placed her hand on mine, trying to get my eyes to meet hers. "You did the right thing, Dex."

"Right," I mumbled.

"Just because..." she trailed off.

I gave her a sharp look. I didn't want her to finish that sentence.

She didn't. She just tapped my hand. "You know you did the right thing. You and Jenn breaking up was long overdue. You deserve someone better than that."

I didn't. But I appreciated the lie.

I smiled quickly and went back to the menu. I was distracting my head with the different toppings I could order when my phone rang.

I shot her an apologetic look and wondered if it was Jimmy. I'd finally talked to him the other day and we discussed my little sabbatical. He was adamant that I keep going with the show anyway and said he had a few tricks up his sleeves—whatever that meant. He probably wanted me to partner up with someone else, and hell, if they didn't see ghosts the way that I supposedly did they'd just fake it. But without Perry, I didn't see a whole lot of point to going forward. Without her, I wanted to do something, anything else.

I fished the phone out of my pocket and quickly glance at the screen. It wasn't Jimmy at all. It was some other number.

My heart stopped beating. I looked at Rebecca.

"Where is area code 503?" I asked quickly.

"Huh?"

"Area code 503!" I repeated in a panic.

Her face grew paler. "Portland."

I couldn't move. I couldn't breathe. Luckily Rebecca snatched the phone out of my hand and answered it for me before the caller hung up.

"Hello?" she asked. She frowned, listening. "Yes he is. May I ask who is calling?"

I bit my lip, my chest growing tight from a lack of oxygen. She looked at me, her eyes wide, her mouth dropping a little bit.

"Hi, Ada. It's Rebecca," she said. "What's going on? Are you okay?"

I immediately put my hand out for the phone. I still wasn't breathing but I was functioning.

She eyed me and nodded. "Okay, calm down, I'm just going to give you to Dex here."

She placed the phone in mine and twitched her head in the direction of the doors. It seemed like it was something I'd need to take in private.

I gave her a quick smile and put the phone to my ear as I got out of the booth.

"Ada?" I asked, making my way past the crowded tables.

"Dex?" I heard her young, tiny voice on the other end.

"Hi, what's up? Is Perry okay?" I didn't want to ask it, I felt like I had no right to, but I couldn't see any other reason for Ada to call. It had been too long since we had our falling out, the time to be reprimanded had passed. And somewhere in my black heart, the minute I asked it, I knew that Perry *wasn't* okay.

I was lucky to have made it out of the restaurant and onto the chilled street when Ada said, "No, she's not okay. Something's happened to her."

I almost dropped the phone. Something had to give, so I did. I leaned against a brick wall and let my legs give out, and slid down until I was sitting on the ground.

"Dex?" she cried out. "Are you there?"

I closed my eyes and swallowed the fear. "Yes. I'm here. What happened?"

"I don't know."

"Is she hurt?" My voice cracked. I swallowed hard, shooting out little prayers in between the answers.

"Not really."

"Ada..."

"I don't know, Dex. I shouldn't even be calling you. I just don't know what to do. I think she's possessed.

She's...she's not herself, I've seen things too, things that are after her. They have her strapped to her bed now."

"Who are they?"

"My parents. Maximus."

"Maximus?!" I roared. People on the street looked at me and quickened their pace as they went past. I didn't care. The rage was almost uncontrollable. "What the fuck is he doing there?"

"He and Perry are, well I don't know. He's a douchecanoe, that's all that matters. Dex, she's gone. She's going. I don't know what to do. We did a house cleanse and then Maximus turned his back on us and is making it look like Perry is crazy. I'm afraid they're going to put her away. You know, in a crazy house. But the thing is killing her, Dex, it's *killing* her."

I was vaguely aware of the restaurant door opening and Rebecca coming out of it. She stood beside me but I couldn't look up at her. I couldn't move. I couldn't even process what was going on. Something had Perry and it was killing her. Something so bad that Ada had to call me—of all people—and ask for *my* help.

"I'll do whatever I can," I told her, trying to get the determination in my voice heard over the phone. "You have to promise to keep her safe until I get there."

"What if I can't? They don't listen to me. They've got her like an animal...and she is an animal, she's an animal now!" Ada broke off as her words got clogged by the tears. Ada was one tough teen cookie. Little Fifteen. To hear her cry over Perry put the final dagger into my heart.

"Ada, listen to me. I'm going to take care of this, okay? I'm not going to let anything else happen to her, you understand me? I am going to do whatever it takes to make sure she gets out of this. Give me a day, give me a few hours, I will be there and I will fix her. You understand, Little Fifteen?"

I heard a sniffle and a pause. Finally she said, "Okay. But please hurry."

"I'll text you when I'm on my way," I told her.

"Thank you. Thank you, Dex," she said. "I knew you weren't as big of an asshole as everyone said."

Oh, gee thanks.

"Yeah, well, we'll see. Hold tight, okay?"

"Okay, bye."

I never made out my bye before the line went dead. I looked up at Rebecca, who was watching me in horror. I was shaking all over.

"I have to go to Perry," I told her, voice wavering. "She's in trouble."

Her eyes widened and then she helped me to my feet before people started thinking I was a crazy street punk.

"Anything I can do?" she asked. I saw the fright in her face and realized how hard it must've been to care about us both.

I couldn't have felt like more of an ass. More of a horrible human being. Not even. A pig, as Rebecca had said. But I couldn't let myself dwell on it anymore either. I had months of that under my belt. I wanted to better myself. This was the best chance for me to prove myself. It wouldn't undo anything but...I couldn't live with myself if I did nothing. Like it or not—and I certainly didn't like it sometimes—Perry was still the most important thing in the world to me. Knowing she was out there was painful enough. But knowing she might not ever be out there again...that was something I couldn't live with.

I shook my head and took Rebecca's hand and kissed it. "Thank you for being there for me through all of this. I've got a few phone calls and bribes to make, then I'm out of here."

"You'll get her back," she said, even though she couldn't have known what trouble Perry was in. "Then when you do, you're going to bring her here and we'll all have pizza together."

I promised her and ran off down the street, into the dusk.

Though Ada's plea was somewhat vague, I wasn't about to take any chances. If she said something had Perry and was killing her, that Maximus—THAT DOUCHE-FUCKER—was there and had to do a house cleansing, I had no choice but to believe that she was possessed. It sounded like something straight out of a movie, something that didn't happen in real life, but I was well-versed in things that voided reality.

The problem was, for a supposed ghost hunter, I had no idea what to do. I'd never felt so god damn helpless before. My first instinct was to just go to Perry and figure it out from there. But that's what the old Dex would have done. I didn't want to show up unprepared, unable to do anything. I wanted a plan. I wanted to save the day.

"Think, you ass," I said out loud as I barged into the apartment. Fat Rabbit jumped off the couch and ran toward me, then took one look at my harried face and went back the way he came.

I ran over to the den and hopped on the internet, even though I knew searching for an exorcist wasn't going to be as easy as I thought. A few chilling pages came up, case stories, the kind of stuff that made you turn around in your chair to see if someone else was in the room with you. It was all so disheartening, really, knowing this shit was going on and knowing that most of the time, no one believed it. You'd think it would make me feel better to know that people like me and Perry weren't alone in this world, but it didn't.

But the Roman Catholic Church didn't seem all that open to exorcisms and few priests would do it. I didn't have time to go around playing Select-a-Priest—I needed someone now. I didn't care if I was overreacting, though I had an inkling I wasn't. "She's an animal now, she's an animal." Ada's words floated in my head, making my gut twist painfully.

Then something caught my eye. Apparently priests weren't the only people to deal with demon or ghost possessions. Native Americans were used to dealing with this kind of crazy shit and that was a culture I at least knew a little bit about. Or, I at least knew someone from it.

I whipped out my phone and started going through my contact list. There it was: Bird Man.

The last time I talked to Old Man Bird was in Red Fox, New Mexico. He was a man I trusted, a man who knew way more than he ever let on. A wise old fuck, if you will. He would know what to do, and if he could do anything, he would help us. Or at least help Perry. They had enjoyed a grandfather/granddaughter kinship, and if I may sound a bit new agey, a slightly spiritual connection.

Hoping for the best, I pushed *call* and put the phone to my ear. It rang a few times and I was starting to wonder if it was too late for me to call him when the line picked up.

"Hello?" Bird's stoic voice answered.

"Hi, Bird? This is Dex Foray, we met back in Red Fox last October…"

"Dex," he pronounced my name slowly. "I knew it was you."

"Oh," I said, taken aback. Shit, maybe he was more new agey than I thought. "Could you sense me?"

"No, I have caller ID," he answered simply. "What seems to be the problem, Dex? It's getting late here and I assume you aren't calling me to talk about life on the ranch. Though, I will tell you, things have calmed down since Sarah and Shan were found."

The skinwalkers. A part of me wanted to hear what happened, get some closure to a story that brought Perry and I so close to death, but there just wasn't time.

"That's great, Bird," I told him. "But I'm afraid I have another problem. A bigger problem. It's about Perry."

"Perry?" His voice grew more alert. "What happened to her?"

I rubbed at my forehead, feeling like a total idiot for not having the right answer. "I don't really know...I haven't seen her for a long time. But her sister called me. She said she's... it's like she's possessed or something. She's strapped to her bed like an animal..." My voice choked and broke off. "I think they're going to try and put her away. But Perry isn't crazy, we know that."

There was a pause, and in that pause I felt all my hopes fading. Then he said, "Tell me again exactly what her sister said. And tell me why you haven't seen her for so long."

I sighed, not wanting to get back into this story. Every time I explained what happened between us, I took one step closer to the darkness, the madness. I had to get past that, past our mistakes.

I took a deep breath and explained to him how Perry lived with me for a week, how we explored the mental institute, how we saw Abby, how she switched my medication, how we made passionate love and promptly tore that love apart. I told him of my descent, my downward spiral, and how I was working to get out of it. I told him she was the light in my madness and I would do absolutely anything to keep her shining.

At the end of all that, instead of feeling the guilt and shame that I normally felt, I felt alive and determined. Maybe I was growing up. Maybe.

"All right," Bird said. "We need to help her. I think I know who can. There's a man in Lapwai, Idaho, who has done this sort of thing before. His name is Roman. It's just there's a very high risk that things can go wrong, do you understand that, Dex? I can't completely vouch for him, and if I feel the situation can't be helped, we can back out. But I feel like he's our only shot. I can feel the urgency in your voice and I can feel it in my bones."

Risk or not, if he was our only shot, we had to take it. "I understand. Let's do it. Is he an exorcist?"

"He's a medicine man. Don't worry, one of the good guys, from the Nez Perce tribe. He was involved in a demon possession case involving a little boy."

"And what happened? Did it work?"

Silence. "The boy died," Bird said.

"Okay, so how about we look at option B."

"There is no option B. This is the most I can do for you at this hour. I haven't even called him yet; he might not even be open to it. But I feel that this is the option we have to take. Like I said, if things get rough, we can back out. But Perry isn't a little boy. She's got age and fight and spirit on her side. If anyone can handle this, it is her."

He was right about that, even though the risk was bigger than I originally thought.

"Dex, we'll do whatever we can," he continued reassuringly. "I'll call you back after I hear from him."

He hung up the phone and I sat back in the chair, pulling my hair out at the sides. I was so damn close to freaking out. I eyed my book of pills, wondering if taking a few of the smuggled-in Valium would help me out. But I needed to think. I needed to be alert and ready to act. I couldn't medicate or drink my way out of this one. Perry needed me more than I needed relief.

I sent a quick text to Ada, asking for an update on the situation. Nothing had really changed, which was great, but it looked like she'd be taken away by morning. She'd been eavesdropping on her parent's conversations and they were adamant that Perry was having a mental breakdown and needed professional help. She said they never believed her, no matter how much Ada backed her up.

I told her I'd be there in a few hours, that I was just waiting on something. I did not want to mention the exorcism, because even though Ada had brought up the idea of possession, it didn't mean she'd be open to the idea of a medicine man doing some magic on her sister. People had different limits when it came to what their brain could accept, I knew this all too well.

Finally, after I paced a mini-marathon around the apartment, Fat Rabbit staring at me with concern, my phone rang.

"Bird!" I exclaimed as I answered, my chest squeezing around my lungs and heart and everything else I considered vital.

"Roman said he'll do it," Bird said. "I have his address here. I'm going to fly to Idaho tonight to help him get ready."

"Oh, you don't have to do that," I told him, touched by his generosity. Bird was a ranch hand from a poor reserve in

New Mexico. He did not have money for an impromptu flight.

"It's no bother," he said, and he somehow made me believe it. "I've already made my reservation. I have to hurry to Albequerque now, you just go to Perry and get her out of there. And be careful."

"I owe you one," I told him.

"You already owed me one," he joked softly. Then he gave me the address and some vague directions that sounded simple enough and said goodbye. That man. I really needed to order him a high-class hooker for his next birthday or something. You know, as a way to say thank you.

I exhaled, steadying myself, and texted Rebecca. I asked her to take care of Fat Rabbit while I was gone and that I'd let her know if there were any developments.

Then I went to the door, not bothering to pack anything. I had my wallet and my car keys; it was all I needed. I stopped by the mirror in the hallway, and at first glance, I hardly recognized myself. For the first time I really saw the differences in my body. My face was skinnier, now covered in a layer of scruff that I didn't shave every day. My arms and shoulders had expanded. I shrugged on my cargo jacket and noticed that even that didn't fit the same as it used to.

Did this mean I was a new man? I didn't know. Perhaps not yet. Perhaps it wasn't a quick fix and a matter of working out and eating right and embracing the crazy fucking nutjob that I was. Still, I decided to take out my eyebrow ring and placed it in my jacket pocket. Now I looked different. And hopefully, different enough for Perry to put her trust in me. I didn't want to be *that* guy anymore, the one that hurt her. I wanted to be me. Perhaps the same me she had seen underneath all this time.

SIX

I sped the Highlander down the I-5 like a demon in the night. Perhaps that was a bad analogy, but I felt almost supernatural as I managed to clock record speeds while somehow avoiding every single speed trap there was out there. I was motherfucking Batman and timing seemed to be on my side—I just hoped it would be as kind to Perry.

I texted Ada as I drove, letting her know I was on my way and urging her to keep things as secret as possible. I was pretty sure that their parents wouldn't be too happy to have me in their house and would probably throw me out on my ass, especially when I decided to quiz them on my dear old Pippa. And Max, well, I had a bad feeling about him. I didn't understand how it was even possible that the giant ginger king was there, in Portland, in their house, meddling in what used to be my affairs. After everything that he and I had been through, this just reeked of sabotage.

It was raining steadily and dark as fuck outside when I turned the car onto Perry's street. As much as I tried to tell myself that everything would be fine and that the plan would work, I was a nervous pervous. I was not only afraid of what was happening to Perry, afraid that I might fail in saving her, but I was afraid of her in general. Not of the thing that had apparently taken over her, but of her. Of what she'd think of me. Of the way she'd look at me.

Christ, I was in over my head and my head was over my heels. I was just a fucking tumbleweed in love with a constant breeze at my back. I slammed the car into park a few houses up from hers, and wished I had a whole packet of Nicorette that I could jam into my mouth.

Alas, I didn't. So I settled for one—bite, bite, chew, then sent one last text to Ada and waited for five painful, agonizing minutes before I saw her lithe little form running down the street through the rain. She jumped in the passenger seat and slammed the door, her white blonde hair going all Debbie Harry on her.

"Hey," I told her, twisting in my seat to get a better look at her. Maybe I should have been afraid of Ada instead of Perry. Though she was just fifteen, Ada looked years older at that moment, dark circles under her eyes, which were wide and flashing like blue hazard lights. She looked jacked up, angry and scared all rolled into one emo bundle. "Thanks for—"

Smack.

It wasn't as hard as Rebecca's slap and from the surprised look on Ada's face, I could tell it was the first time she hit someone and meant it, but damn. The Palominos had some serious anger management issues. Or Dex Foray issues. Potatoes, po*tat*oes.

I stretched out my jaw and shot her a wary look. "Well, I suppose I deserved that."

"I thought about it and decided you're still an asshole," she snarled. Then smiled politely. "But thank you for coming."

Oh man, what did I get myself into? Nope, didn't matter. I'd walk over hot coals and a million teenage slaps if it meant getting to Perry.

"You're probably going to get it worse from my dad," she went on. Okay, make that a million teenage slaps and a punch from an angry Italian.

"Let's try and prevent that from happening. Anyway, can you sneak me into her room?"

She shook her head. "Maximus is in there, thinking he's taking care of her. He's such a tool."

I ground my teeth together, not appreciating the mental image of Perry strapped to a bed with Max taking "care" of her.

"Well, the flannel-coated pussy stealer won't be taking care of her for much longer," I said, unbuckling my seatbelt. She looked at me blankly. Perhaps she didn't appreciate her sister being referred to as "pussy." I cleared my throat. "I meant flannel-coated...ginger douche."

She dipped her chin and said dryly, "Dude, the term is douchecanoe."

She flung her door open and we ran down the street in the pouring rain. The Palominos' large house loomed at the end of their driveway, the lights from the windows looking more like reptilian eyes than anything else. Warm and cozy? Nuh-uh. I could already tell that something was terribly wrong and I felt it in every part of my body. Evil? Yeah, I could believe evil lived in that house.

A movement at Perry's window caught my eye—the silhouette of he-who-shall-not-be-named-except-in-insults-I-found-fitting. My fists clenched and I breathed out slowly through my nose. So many things were rushing through me —conflicting, dangerous feelings, it was no wonder Ada looked so torn and cracked out. My head and heart were already being done in and I hadn't even been in the house yet.

We paused on the steps, Ada holding her finger to her mouth, as if I needed to be quiet. Maybe I was breathing through my nose rather loudly.

"Just stay behind me," she whispered. "I think my parents are in their room."

I nodded and she pushed the door open. I was immediately met with this...darkness. A malevolence, like a cancer in the air, that rushed through me, making me feel sick all over.

Ada gave me a look like she understood exactly what I was going through and I followed her in, walking as quietly as possible. I shrugged off my wet jacket, a droplet of water running down my neck.

It was strangely still inside, like some unseen life force inside had paused the second I walked in. It's hard to explain, but since I was grasping for the impossible anyway, it was almost like there was a fuck-you-up energy in the house that was waiting in a hidden corner somewhere, ready to pounce.

"You feel it too?" she asked quietly, as we walked up the stairs, my eyes searching the dark hallway that led to even darker rooms.

I nodded. "Is it always like this?"

She shook her head. "I can feel it, all the time. But it's never been so calm like this. It's freaking me the fuck out."

"Like it knows I'm here."

We exchanged a worried glance and continued up the stairs, the blood pounding more loudly in my head the closer I got to the top.

Once there, I could see Perry's room at the end, the door slightly ajar. I could hear his stupid drawl but couldn't make out what he was saying. We walked to the door and Ada slowly pushed it open, casting me a furtive glance before doing so. As if she was trying to prepare me.

Maximus was standing in front of Perry, looking down at her. I couldn't really see her body, but I could tell she was lying on the bed, immobile. A rope was wrapped around one leg and down around the bed post. I focused on her foot, her little toes, the fact that she was held down. I couldn't even move. I could only listen as he went on, not noticing either me or Ada in the doorway.

"Just get through tonight," he said in an overly cloying voice. "Things will turn around tomorrow."

"And what will you do when the men in the white coats take me away?" Perry answered. I hadn't heard her voice in so fucking long. I almost collapsed right there and then, her presence rolling through me, wanting to bring me to my knees like she had before. "What will you say then? Will you still ask me if I'm scared?"

She sounded so small, so afraid. It speared me.

"Wherever you end up, Perry, it'll be for the best," Maximus said. I couldn't believe his fucking audacity. "They'll make you new again. The doctors will help you. They'll treat you. You'll be given medicine and it'll fix you. Those mental institutions have a bad rap, you know that. But they do more good than harm, especially for people like you. It may be scary at first, but you'll be fixed. You'll be as good as new."

I couldn't let this happen. He was full of absolute shit. What the fuck did he know about being diagnosed with a mental disorder? Nothing. *Nothing*.

But I did.

I cleared my throat, the anger boiling up. "Are you sure about that, *Max*?"

Maximus flinched, startled, and whipped his head toward me. His jaw came unhinged, his face pale with disbelief. That's right, you red nutsack. Guess who's here? Your worst nightmare.

Ada brushed past me and walked around the foot of the bed, her eyes on Perry, trying to give her fair warning for my appearance.

"What in God's name are *you* doing here?" he exclaimed, blinking hard as if I were an apparition. He'd be so lucky. A ghost wouldn't kick his fucking ass the way I could.

But I couldn't concentrate on him. He was only part of the problem. I was here because of Perry, and as he moved over, straightening up to look at me dead on, he revealed Perry on the bed behind him.

And my whole world stopped.

It barely even looked like her. I mean, it *was* her. Her beautiful, petite face that was so easy to cup in my hands, her long black hair cloaking her like a shield. Her breasts as they filled out her sweater, somehow even bigger than before. But her eyes didn't look the same, her expression was shocked, just as shocked as I was, but something didn't match up.

It didn't matter though. Nothing mattered at that moment except for the fact that the love of my life was in emotional and physical pain, strapped to her own bed, very much like the animal that Ada had said she was. A million things passed between us—love, anger, regret, sorrow. They flew faster than anyone could see, in a language all our own, between my dark eyes and her dark eyes. No, that was it. Her eyes. They weren't her eyes. They belonged to someone else. My god, what the fuck was going on here? What happened to her?

I snapped. I charged right up to the first person I could blame.

"What the fuck is this?" I yelled in Maximus's face, throwing my arms around. "What are you doing to her?"

"What the fuck is this? What the fuck are you? Why are you here? You shouldn't be here!" the Douchefucker yelled back, not backing down, as if he had the right to be mad and not me.

"You should thank your freckled ass that I'm here," I sniped, coming closer. Did he think I was afraid of him, because I was about to show him how a *real* mentally deranged person behaved.

"Guys!" Ada yelled. She then looked at Perry nervously. "It's okay, I invited him."

"Why would you do a stupid thing like that?" Maximus said to her. Oh, I was so damn close to feeding him his own dick.

"Stupid?" Ada cried out, her hair flying. "I'm not going to sit back and let you tie *my* sister to her own bed, pretend you know what the hell is going on with her, and then cart her off to a hospital tomorrow when we all know she's probably not going to be coming back!"

As nice as it was to see Little Fifteen acting so supportive of her sister—especially when I knew how strained their relationship could be at times—she wasn't my concern. Perry was watching everyone, her eyes darting between the three of us until they rolled back in her head and it slumped into the pillow. She started to twitch. Oh Jesus.

I took a few steps closer, wanting to touch her, to hold her. This couldn't be possession. This had to be something else. "What's wrong with her?" I asked.

"I'd stay away if I were you, son," Maximus said, putting his arm out to stop me.

Son? I bit down on my lip to keep from saying something I really wanted to say and threw his arm off of me. I went over to her and crouched down so that I was at her level. Her head rolled back and forth, as if she was arguing with herself inside.

"She's not well," I said stupidly. Did she even *really* know I was here?

"No shit, Sherlock," said Maximus.

Her eyes opened for a second, looking at me blankly. Just as I thought, they weren't hers. They were brown. "Did you notice her eyes are a different color?" I asked Maximus, practically seething at his ignorance.

He snorted. "What are you talking about? No they aren't, they're just dilated."

I shook my head, fighting my anger. "Dilated but the color around them is brown now. Perry's eyes have always been blue. Like the ocean on an overcast day."

Ada gasped. "Dex is right."

Of course I was fucking right. And I wasn't about to stand here and take this. I reached for the ropes, starting to untie them, wincing at how raw her delicate skin was. I swallowed hard, trying to keep focused and calm, to hold my emotions at bay. I had to get through this, for both of us.

"Dex, don't do that," Maximus warned. "She's tied up for a reason, not for sport."

"She's not a fucking animal," I grunted, ignoring him.

Suddenly, Perry raised her head. "I wouldn't do that if I were you," she said in a quiet voice.

I looked at her just as the last knot came undone and our eyes met. I looked deep into her strange new soul. She had to know I was here to help her, not to harm her. I was trying to *save* her. "It's me, Perry. It's Dex."

She smiled at me. It was chilling.

"*Precisely*." A depraved, gravelly voice came out from her raised lips. Not her voice. Not even a human one.

Before I could even process what was happening, she lunged forward out of the ropes and grabbed me by my shirt. Her hands almost burned into me and the smell of sulfur momentarily filled my nose before she flung me across the room. One minute I was at the bed, the next I was thrown, landing on the ground, pain shooting up from my shoulder.

Ada was at my side but it didn't matter because Perry, that thing that was inside her, broke free out of the rest of the ropes like Bruce Banner on crystal meth. She leaped, fucking *leaped*, in the air and tackled me back to the ground. I saw nails coming after my eyes and shut them hard before she could get at them. She scratched at them anyway, the skin growing wet with my blood, before she went after my throat, wrapping her burning fingers around it.

I couldn't breathe. Whoever this was, she was a hell of a lot stronger than me. Devastatingly stronger than me. My heart beat hard as I struggled for breath, my limbs feeling numb as her grip somehow tightened. Her beautiful and deadly face was growing dim as my eyes couldn't stay open.

But this couldn't be it. She had to know, even if she hated me so much, she had to know it was me. That I meant something to her at some point. That she meant everything to me.

I managed to open them again, trying to focus on her, trying to get her to see me.

I don't know if it worked or not, but I swear I saw a flash of her somewhere in those dark caverns. She hesitated for a second, her grip loosening, and in that second she was grabbed by Maximus and ripped off of me.

She cried out, an ungodly noise, as her legs flailed above the ground, trying to fight him. Okay, despite all the crazy ass shit that was suddenly going on, I felt a tiny bit emasculated by the fact that he had no problem containing her super-villain strength.

"Ada, the rope," he commanded.

Ada was leaning over me, trying to see if I was alive. That was nice of her.

"Leave him. Get the rope," he boomed. "Get it now!"

Ada jumped up and snatched the ropes off the bed.

And just like that, Perry suddenly fell limp in his arms and Ada hesitantly started winding the rope around her.

"No, onto the bed," he said to her. They brought Perry to the bed and started tying her up. Despite what happened, I still couldn't believe it.

I got unsteadily to my feet, feeling around my throat. It hurt to touch, as did each breath I took. How could she have done that to me? I expected a slap, like the one everyone else had given me. Maybe even a kick in the balls. But this... what was I saying about being over my head and head over heels? She meant business and I had no fucking clue what I was going to do. How the hell was I going to get her to Lapwai to get a god damn exorcism when she seemed to have this new desire to kill me?

Ada came to my side. "Do you want some ice?" she asked gently.

I shook my head, unable to look away from Perry's tired expression, afraid that if I did so, I'd never see the real her again. I didn't even know who I was looking at.

Maximus folded his arms like he was cock of the

fucking walk and strolled into my vision. "I told you so. You're going to have a heck of a mark on your face there."

I eyed him suspiciously. It just sunk in that he had a similar looking scratch on his face, as if Perry had clawed him too.

I coughed, trying to clear my lungs. "That how you got yours?"

"She's feisty."

I didn't like his tone. My eyes narrowed some more. "I guess we'll match then."

Maximus chuckled to himself. I knew exactly what that laugh meant. It was the condescending, *oh Dex, you don't get it, do you* laugh.

"Not quite," he said and winked at me.

Okay, I definitely didn't get it now, and what was more troubling was that he wanted me to get it. And as stupid as I was, I decided to barrel on in.

"What's that supposed to mean?" I asked carefully.

Maximus shrugged and ran his hand through his carrot top. "Oh, nothing," he teased.

He moseyed to the end of the bed and leaned against the bed post across from me, copying my stance. He smiled, slowly, and way too fucking surely. "I just had no idea she was such a wildcat in the sack."

What?

"Oh, it wasn't like that with you?" he asked innocently.

Ada cried out. "What? Maximus!" But I barely heard her. All I heard was my blood pressure whooshing through my body, building into my fists.

I raised my brow, almost unable to comprehend it. "Excuse me?"

Maximus' smile grew wider. He looked like a fucking redneck Archie Andrews.

"You heard me," he said delicately, his eyes blazing into mine like he owned the world. "She's a freaky little one. Good thing I kind of like it rough."

Wildcat in the sack. He liked it rough.

Perry had scratched him during sex.

Perry had slept with Maximus.

He stuck his dick in her.

I was going to be sick.

I was going to cry.

Oh, wait. No, I was going to BEAT THE LIVING SHIT OUT OF HIM!

I didn't even need to fully wind up, I just exploded, my fist making contact with his jaw. My knuckles exploded in pain but fuck it hurt so good. It even sounded good, that crack of bone, the wet sound of lips and gums being smashed together. He went stumbling backward from my fist, falling onto Perry's desk, bringing it all down underneath him.

Perry and Ada were yelling. Frankly, my dears, I didn't give a shit. I was going to destroy this motherfucker if it was the last thing I did. I would beat the mental image of them together out of his head.

Before the rat bastard could get back up, I jumped on him. I clocked him in the cheekbone then went for the other side of his jaw, landing a sharp uppercut. I tried to get him in the nose, something I so desperately wanted to break, but the fury that was rolling out of me was almost blinding. I was rage incarnate and I delivered punch after punch after punch.

More cries filled the room, and I knew the jig was up. I felt arms grab me roughly from behind and haul me off of Maximus, who was rolling on the floor, grabbing his face.

Suddenly Ada was in front of me, her hands on my

chest, pushing me further back into whom I could only assume was Perry's father.

"Enough!" she cried out. "This isn't helping Perry! That's not why you're here. Remember."

She put her face right up to mine, forcing me to meet her eyes. She was pleading, desperately, trying to remind me why I was there. I did remember. I had to save Perry. I couldn't screw it up now, no matter how badly I wanted to kill Maximus. Not just for screwing her, but for allowing all of this to happen. He should have been on her side.

I bit my lip and nodded that I understood, then I closed my eyes to the scene just as Perry's father dug his hands into my arm and pulled me across the room. Oh boy, I was in deep shit now with Mr. Mafia.

"What on earth is going on?" her father yelled, his eyes boring into Perry and Ada's. He gave me a disgusted look and a dismissive push that I was jonesing to retaliate. "Why is *he* here?"

"Dad!" Perry yelled at him, seemingly normal again. Or maybe this was all a trick.

"I called him," Ada quickly explained and walked over to me. I hoped this was a sign of solidarity because I didn't have a very fair fight against Tony Soprano, Ginger Elvis, *and* the Ice Queen. "I thought he could help."

"You called *him* of all people?" Her dad jabbed his thumb in my direction. I held back my shoulders, hoping my new body was at least slightly intimidating. Didn't he see what I did to Maximus' face?

He glared, not relenting in the slightest. "After what you did to my daughter, you should be glad I'm merely going to kick you out of my house."

Huh. How interesting. "How about what you did? Your

little daughter there is tied to her own bed. She's sick and getting sicker by the minute."

"She's going to the hospital first thing in the morning." I was surprised he didn't roll his eyes.

I took a step toward him. He didn't get it at all. He *needed* to get it.

"If you take her there," I said, all steel and sharp edges, "you will kill her. You have no idea what you are dealing with here."

My father didn't move. "Oh, I'm sorry, I didn't realize you had a plan."

I looked at everyone. "I do have a plan."

"Well it's too bad you can't stay to tell us about it," he said snidely. He put his hands on my shoulders and began pushing me toward the door.

Like I was going to go that easily.

I stopped suddenly and looked over at Maximus who was rubbing his jaw, looking all butthurt. Aw, poor baby.

I turned to face her dad, his round face under round glasses, eyes that were burning with anger. It's touching that he wanted to protect his daughter so badly, but he was going about this the completely wrong way.

"It's funny that you both don't remember me," I said.

Her dad shot her mother a confused look. Not that Perry's mom ever looked anything *but* confused.

"We've met before," I went on with a smile. "Back in New York. I was just a young fuck at the time. I had a deadbeat, alcoholic crazy bitch of a mother and a wonderful nanny. She was a bit loopy too..."

"We don't know what you're talking about," he said. I think I believed him. But her mother. No, no, she got it. She understood. She knew exactly who I was. And who Pippa was.

I took a step toward the blonde pillar and grinned wickedly. It was wrong of me to be relishing this, but I was.

"When I turned eighteen, I changed my last name to my mother's name. To honor her death. Guess I was sentimental back then. Before that, my name was Declan O'Shea."

Her dad's eyes widened. Oh, *now* he knew. He gave me another push by way of response. "You need to get out of here. Now."

"Such a rush?" I asked, slowly letting him take me out the door.

"I have no problem calling the cops on you," he responded. I knew he would, too. I didn't want to push it that far, but it was fun seeing how upset they were. I really got to them. For once, I sort of had the upper hand.

"No really," I said, as we went down the stairs with Maximus and Queen Bitch trailing behind. "I'm surprised Perry doesn't talk more about her grandmother. She does know about her, doesn't she? Her...condition?"

"Out!" her father yelled again, pointing at the front door. Maximus stood beside him for backup, but even though his face was battered from my fists, he looked doubtful. Wary even, of the people he was standing with. And Perry's mother? Well I could see she was just crumbling from the fear. I didn't even really *know* what I knew, but I knew I had struck a chord with her, right where it hurt.

I paused by the door and raised my hands in the air. "Hey, I came here to make amends and to try and help your daughter. If you all can't see that, then you'll end up suffering for the consequences."

Then I turned around and ran out into the night.

SEVEN

I GOT IN MY CAR AND DROVE OFF THROUGH THE RAIN. I didn't go very far, just to the next street over where I texted Bird and warned him that we might be a bit later than what we had planned on. Then I sent a message to Ada, saying I wasn't actually going anywhere and that I'd sneak back later. I never got a response, so I assumed she was talking with Perry or her parents. I could only hope to hell that Ada wouldn't cave in and spoil everything. It couldn't be easy living in that house, and I wouldn't blame her for wanting to keep the peace, even if her love for Perry was greater.

While I waited, I rested my head on the steering wheel and kept replaying the images of the night through my head. It was terrible. It was like a car accident you couldn't stop staring at, a movie where you're too afraid to look away from the screen. I saw Perry, my beautiful, strong Perry, reduced to a shell. She was being held prisoner in her own body, only allowed to come out on occasion. And she had to fight for it, I could tell. She was dying inside and no one was helping her. Everyone she loved and trusted had turned against her.

Including me. I was here to help her but the damage had already been done and it was done by my own hand. When Rebecca had told me how bitter and angry Perry was, I believed it. And now I believed it went much deeper than that. This thing inside of her was feeding on her rage, the rage I created. I made the monster.

My eyes stung hot with tears that thankfully never fell. I couldn't handle this. I handled so much before but I couldn't handle this. Not like this. Not now. Seeing her, being with her...it only drove the knives deeper into my stomach. And knowing she slept with Maximus, picturing her riding him, kissing him, being intimate with him...the knives twisted. My soul was bleeding and the pain wouldn't stop. It just kept coming, soaking me with red despair. I wanted to scream, I want to hit Maximus some more, I wanted to yell at Perry and ask her why she'd do that to me. Then I wanted to hit myself, yell at myself, destroy myself because I was the reason.

That's how I spent the night. Waiting in the darkness, the rain falling on the roof, hoping there was still time to make things right.

It was about two in the morning when I decided to give it a go. I started the car and drove back around the corner and down Perry's street. I parked it just out of sight of their house and checked my phone for any last minute texts. There was nothing. Ada still hadn't gotten back to me.

It didn't matter. I'd make a go of it on my own. I got out of the car and crept toward the house. Her bedroom light was off, which was a good sign. She was probably alone. I spied the tree that rather conveniently reached toward the roof and her window. That would do.

A month or two ago, I would have hung from it like a monkey, but now thanks to countless sessions on the pull-up bar, I was able to climb the tree with ease. I quietly stepped onto the roof then moved across the shingles until I was just outside her window.

I peeked in. It was dark but there was just enough light coming from a charging phone in the corner. Perry was lying in bed, still strapped in. I took a deep breath and tried to get the window open. It took a few attempts, and in my impatience, I almost put my fist through it, but in the end it slid open, clattering too loudly in the frame.

Perry's shape stirred on the bed then froze. "Hey, kiddo," I whispered. "It's just me."

I fucking hoped it was her.

I quickly climbed through the window and made my way over to the bed. I crouched to her level and she turned her head on the pillow to face me. She looked okay, like herself again.

And I realized that was just as fucking frightening. Because if the real Perry wanted to kill me, that was something I couldn't just recover from.

I was rattled beyond words and tried to give her a smile.

"Sweet climbing tree you've got there," I said, nodding outside, grasping for conversation. What to say? What could I possibly say to her, now, after all this time?

I looked back at her, at the way she was looking at me, open yet guarded. She looked so weak, so torn and ravaged. "How are you?"

"How do you think?" she asked.

"Yeah," I said, smiling softer now. "I know. I'm going to get you out of here, okay?"

"Where?"

"I said I had a plan. Your parents never gave me a chance to tell it to them. You just have to trust me."

She glared at me. I missed that glare. "How the fuck do you think I can trust you?"

Ouch. This wasn't going to be easy. I rubbed anxiously at my face, hoping she'd trust me enough to see this through. "I deserve that, I know. And I don't blame you. But none of that's important right now. Later, yes. Not now, kiddo. Ada was right. You can't stay here. Whatever's inside you, it's going to kill you. Sooner rather than later. And a hospital, alone…Perry you don't want to die in there."

Her eyes widened. Now she was getting it, what everyone else wasn't.

I reached over and gently ran my fingers down her hand. Her skin was still so smooth, so soft. I battled inside to keep my focus where it needed to be. She needed comfort, she needed to know she was going to be okay. I stared into her eyes, finding her inside them. "It's true. I'm not trying to scare you. In fact, you're the one who's scaring me. As usual. But we have to go." I took a deep breath. "Will you come with me?"

I asked her like the world didn't depend on it. But my world did.

She seemed to think about it first. "You'll have to untie me."

"I'll risk it."

"Promise you'll tie me up again after?"

That was the last thing I wanted to do. I didn't want to become like her family. I couldn't treat her that way, no matter what she had done.

"I don't want to."

"But you have to," she pleaded. "Or I won't go. I don't want to hurt you again."

"Even though I deserve it?"

"You deserve something. But not that."

I breathed in deeply. I didn't have much choice here. "Okay, deal."

I leaned over and slowly untied her left arm. I was so close to her now, closer than I'd been so far. She didn't quite smell the same—it was a far cry from the shampoo scent I used to smell on the sheets. But there was this musk, this primal essence of her that came off her skin. It was there, pushing through the mask. It gave me hope.

And, if we're being honest here, a bit of a boner.

Now's not the time, I told myself and concentrated on getting her free.

Her hand came free first and she wiggled the feeling back into it while I untied the other. With her entire upper body free, I was bit wary. If she was going to bite my face off like some bath salt junkie, there wouldn't be much I could do about it.

She shot me a knowing smile. "I'm okay."

I nodded, chewing on my lip before I untied her legs. When I finished, I gently slid my arm underneath her back and lifted her up into a sitting position.

"Here, up you go. Easy...take it easy." She was weak as anything but fuck it felt good to be touching her again.

She twitched a bit and started rubbing at her temples. I cupped the back of her head, so small in my hand, and tried to support her. She shut her eyes and pointed at the rope I had just freed her from.

"Tie me up," she said, her voice straining.

"Right now?" I just undid her.

"Please, Dex."

I sighed and reluctantly started wrapping the rope around her wrists and ankles. I trusted her to know when things were going to get rough, but it pained me to do this to her. I couldn't even pretend that this was something kinky, that's how far gone I was.

"Do it tighter," she admonished me.

See. I couldn't even make that into a joke.

I reached over and tilted her chin up, forcing her to open her eyes and look at me.

"What?" she asked. "You saw what I did. Your throat is practically blue."

Blue throat or not, this was the hardest pill to swallow. Even she didn't trust herself. "I don't like this."

"And I do?"

Her eyes pleaded with me and I had no choice but to do what she asked. I tied them as tight as I could without cutting off her circulation.

"I'm obviously going to have to carry you," I admitted.

"Obviously."

I put my arms behind her back and knees and lifted her up. I had always found it easy to carry Perry, even though her boobs did make up the bulk of her. But now, with the new body, it was much, much easier. Would it be petty to admit I felt cocky at a moment like this? Probably.

She didn't seem to notice or care. She just rested her head into my neck, her breath tickling my skin, and I nearly died inside.

I took a shaky step, then asked if she was okay.

She nodded and I ignored the fact that her lips brushed against my neck as she did so.

"Here goes nothing," I said to myself. I got a better grip of her in my hands, then opened the door to the hall. There was a dim nightlight down the hall near her parents' room, but everything else was dark. I could tell from the way she was tensing up that she couldn't wait to get rid of this house of horrors.

I walked as smoothly and as quietly as I could with her in my arms, making my way down the hall and the stairs. So far so good. We needed luck on our side tonight and had to get out of the house without anyone seeing us. I didn't even know where Maximus was, but it wouldn't have surprised me if he was sleeping on the living room couch like the traitorous freeloader that he was.

Step by step, we made it to the hardwood floors. The front door was so close.

But we weren't alone.

A dark figure approached us until the light from upstairs illuminated her eyes.

Ada. Still fully clothed, like she'd been waiting for us.

"What are you doing with her?" she hissed.

"I'm taking her. This is part of the plan."

"Taking her where? You never told me the plan."

"You guys, shut up!" Perry whispered harshly. "You'll wake Maximus."

She jerked her head in the direction of the living room.

So I was right. I went on, lowering my voice even more. "I can't tell you the plan. When your parents find out what I've done—"

"They'll call the fuzz!" she shot in.

"Exactly. And you'll be grilled until you tell them the truth."

"I can keep a secret."

"No she can't," Perry whispered to me. I felt a surge of warmth at her sudden camaraderie and had to hide my smile.

"See, Perry knows. Just trust me, Ada. You called me here for a reason, didn't you? I'm saving your sister the only way I know how."

"And how is that?"

The million dollar question.

"She needs an exorcist."

Exorcist. The word seemed to bounce off the walls as the two of them chewed it over in disbelief.

"An exorcist?" Ada repeated.

"Yes," I said with a sigh. "You know. You've seen the film."

"Actually, I haven't."

Are you kidding me? What was wrong with this girl? "Well, you should. It's very good."

"Guys," Perry whispered again. "Maximus!"

"Please, Ada," I begged her, ready to go into grovel mode. "Just let us go. You know I'll do anything for Perry. She's safer with me than with anyone else."

"My dad will call the cops the minute you're gone," she said, but I could tell she was relenting. "They'll come after you. For, like, kidnapping or something."

"I know." It was worth it.

Ada folded her arms and stuck her leg out in front of her. "Then I'm going with you."

Yeah, so I can get two kidnapping charges. "No. This is nasty business, Little Fifteen."

"I don't care. There wouldn't even be a dumb plan if it wasn't for me. I'm going with you. She's my sister and you need someone to watch over her while you drive. And if you don't take me with you, I'm just going to march over to your little ginger friend over there and—"

"Fine. You can come. But we're going now. *Right* now. Before it's too late."

She beamed at us in victory then crept quietly to the front door and opened it. With Perry safely in my arms, I ran out into the rain and dark. My feet splashed in the puddles beneath.

As I held her, I whispered into her ear, "I'm just around the corner, a few more seconds."

Ada quietly closed the door behind us, and within seconds she was at our side as we approached the Highlander. She opened the back doors and I gently placed Perry on the seat. Ada hopped in on the other side, choosing to keep Perry company. And maybe keep her in her seat.

I got behind the wheel and eyed them both in the rearview mirror.

"Last chance to get out and live a normal life," I said.

"Are you kidding? I gave that up for Lent," Ada answered, rolling her eyes to the heavens. Perry managed a small smile, and together we sped off down the road to Idaho. One step closer to safety. One step closer to getting Perry back.

IT WAS EARLY MORNING, THE SUN INAPPROPRIATELY bright, when we finally made it to Lapwai. The drive hadn't been an easy one. No, it was the most fucking terrifying drive I ever had to take, and I had to drive with Jenn and her mother for twelve hours once.

We made two pit stops, the first to wrap Perry up in duct tape like a kidnapped worm thanks to her attempt to jump out of the car while we were on the highway. The second involved a swarm of wasps coming out of her. I panicked, thanks to my wasp allergy, and we totally crashed. The car wasn't damaged *too* badly and somehow I wasn't hurt except for a minor blow to my head, but that didn't explain what was happening. She was getting worse, and every time I looked back at her in the mirror, I didn't recognize the person there. Instead there was thing, this malicious, dark and evil thing that seemed more and more familiar by the second. It wanted to destroy me, destroy Ada, and most of all, destroy the host. It wanted Perry dead in the end.

We thought we could get her to hang on just a little while longer, just so she could explain to Bird and Roman what was going on. But at about the time dawn broke over the rugged hills of eastern Washington, the Perry we knew and loved had ceased to exist. Instead, Ada and I were left with this creature that writhed and screamed and spoke in tongues. I didn't know whether to be horrified or angry. At times, I was both.

When we pulled up to the small rancher in the middle of butt fuck nowhere, I nearly collapsed from relief. We used the remaining amount of duct tape to secure her to the seat—she even had a strip over her mouth, to keep her from spewing her venom at us. If she had grown any stronger during the journey, I don't think we would have made it there alive.

A reed-thin native man with small, calculating eyes came out of the old rancher, the door banging back and forth against the wall.

I ran out of the car and approached him.

"Roman?" I asked, holding out my hand.

He shook it, firm and quick, then held it out for Ada.

She shook his hand, looking surprised at how young Roman looked. He was probably in his mid-thirties, tops.

Roman was followed by Bird. Bird looked almost the same as when I last saw him, strong despite the long grey hair, and confident despite the worry lines on his forehead. Seeing him gave me more of a boost. Finally, Ada and I were not alone. Perry was finally going to get the help she needed.

I smiled for the first time in ages. It made the wound on my head sting.

"Dex," he said, giving me a single, hard pat on the shoulder and squeezing it firmly. "I'm so glad you made it. Though, your head..."

I shrugged it off. "Minor car accident. We're fine. But Perry isn't."

He looked over my shoulder at the car and headed straight for it.

I opened the door and Bird peered inside. I could feel him tense up at the sight of little Perry wrapped up in duct tape, breathing violently out of her nose, her eyes batshit crazy and slicing into everyone.

Roman took one look at her and then began muttering something in his native tongue. To my surprise, Bird understood him and answered back. I had a feeling that Perry was too much for Roman to handle and it felt like every hope I had in the world was about to be crushed to death.

"Excuse me?" I asked, trying to hide the rising horror in my voice. "But what's the problem?"

Bird looked at Perry with utter regret, then gave me a tight-lipped smile. "Roman's upset because I didn't tell him how bad she really was."

"I didn't know," I said defensively. I turned to Roman. "I didn't know until last night. You speak English, right?"

"Yes, I speak English," Roman snapped. He waved his hand at Perry dismissively. "She's too far gone; this is unfixable."

No. No. I couldn't believe that. I would not accept that. We didn't come all this way to give up. Perry was fixable. End of story.

I grabbed Roman by the front of his sweatshirt and brought him right up to my face.

"You're going to fix her," I snarled, my eyes piercing into his. "She's a lot stronger than she looks. She is still in there and you're going to help her, or so help me God."

"You'll need your God if you think you're going to win this battle," Roman said. He exchanged a measured look with Bird and then gave me short nod. "Okay. Let's see what we can do. Just, please release me."

Just like that, huh? That seemed a bit too easy. Still, I took my hands off of his sweatshirt and backed off. I shot Perry a quick glance, wishing that she could know what I was trying to do for her, and walked around the car, trying to control my emotions. It was getting to be too much now. We were so close. So damn close.

I could hear Roman and Bird talking to each other in their native tongue as they looked over Perry and I could only hope that Bird was doing what he could to encourage him. Ada was standing by the rancher, wringing her hands together, looking like she was going to lose it at any minute. Poor girl had gone through so much. I regretted bringing her along for her own sake, though she saved my ass a bunch already.

"Hey," I said to her as I stood beside her. "You okay?"

She nodded even though it was quite obvious that we weren't okay. We couldn't be further from being okay. We were down and out and struggling to hold onto hope, hope that was currently looking over Perry like she was a lab specimen.

"Bird will help us," I told her. "He won't give up on her. You'll see."

Ada bit her lip, blinking fast.

"And neither will we," I added. I reached down and grabbed the cold, tiny hand of Little Fifteen and tried to give her the strength that I sure as fuck lacked.

She squeezed back, her eyes wet as she looked at me, pleadingly. "But what if we can't save her? What if it's too late? What if it's all for nothing and we lose her right here in the middle of nowhere?"

I could tell she was having doubts now, doubts about bringing Perry all the way here when maybe she would have been better off at home. Doubts about trusting me, assuming that I knew best. I'd be lying if there wasn't a part of me that was wondering the same thing.

"We're going to get through this," I told her, wishing I could make us both believe it. "All of us."

A monstrous groan came from the car as our attention went back to it. Roman and Bird had a wriggling Perry in their arms, carrying her toward us in a hurry.

I kept the rusted door to the house open as they took her inside. I could feel the waves of animosity rolling off of Perry's body, the hate, the need to win and destroy everything she was inside. It felt colder than the winter wind that was whipping through the sunshine, blanketing us with a sense of defeat.

Ada and I followed close behind, navigating through the small house. It totally looked like a single dude lived here, though, aside from a room that looked like a grow-op, it was hard to tell that the single dude was also an exorcist. Maybe I expected more native, medicine man-type artifacts, but the place was pretty bare, with a lot of dust floating in the air.

They took Perry into a large room with just a bed in the middle and an armchair in the corner. There was a pretty bad ass painting of a raven on the wall but it didn't look very homey or lived in. Still, it was better than a hospital. It had to be.

I began to take that thought back after they placed Perry

down on the bed and Roman brought three leather straps out from under her.

"What are you doing?" I asked, taking a step toward him.

Roman ignored me and went around to the other side, pulling out three more straps. Then he leaned over Perry and started strapping her down, across her chest, hips and legs.

"Is that really necessary?" I exclaimed, about to pounce on him. This was no better than a hospital at all!

Ada reached out and dug her long nails into my arm, pulling me back.

"You know it is," she said quietly, her eyes warning me.

Damn it. She was right. Of course she was right, we had her covered in duct tape—in fact she still was. We had to do what was necessary and Roman was no different. But it didn't mean I had to like it.

Roman took out a pocket knife and snapped the blade out. Ada gasped from beside me but he quickly took the knife and sliced it down Perry's middle. I winced as he did so, afraid that if she moved violently at the wrong moment, she would get hurt. But Roman was quick and soon she was free from her duct tape prison.

"I won't rip it off," he said to her. "I know it would hurt you, still."

"I hope you're talking to Perry," I said.

Roman gave me a grave look. "I am. I can see she's there, too. But you both must understand that I may have to hurt Perry at some point."

Wait a dipshit minute here. I didn't agree to *that*.

"What? No!" Ada protested for the both of us. "You don't hurt her. You hurt what's *in* her."

Roman frowned, eying the both of us with frustration, sticking the knife back in his pocket.

"Sometimes you don't have a choice," he said matter-of-factly.

"Is that what happened with the last boy, the one who died?" I found myself saying, the fury in my voice surprising me.

Roman's eyes grew cold at what I said. Ah shit. Stupid move, Dex. Way to insult the only man who can save her.

"I barely touched the boy," he said, pronouncing his words with deliberation. "He would have died anyway. I did get the demon out and that's what counts. Do you think it's easy to see that happen? He was only four. I had to move towns; everyone was saying I did something wrong. But I didn't. The damage was already done when he came to me. It was too late."

Beneath his anger at me, I could feel the regret and sorrow in his voice. I felt like shit for being so callous. Tension cloaked us as I tried to think of something to say. Luckily Bird came back into the room holding a large box which he placed in front of Roman.

He gave me and Ada a stern, *shape-up-or-ship-out* look. "If Roman seems cold, it's because he has to be. The medicine man can have no emotional attachments to the person in question. He can have no fear. Evil preys on fear. It feeds on emotions. Even love."

Roman started lifting things out of the box. But I wasn't interested in the contents. I was interested in Perry. Because she was watching me. *She* was. Her head was lifted and her eyes were on mine and I was drowning in their depths, not caring if I'd ever come out of them, because, for once, they were her eyes. She was still here. We had a fighting chance.

Then, just like that, I lost her again.

Bird and Roman brought out a small drum, incense holders, little wooden bowls and bags of earth-colored herbs and a bunch of dried plants. Roman looked up at Ada and I and said, "We have to set up for the ceremony. You will have to leave the room."

I shook my head. "I don't think so." Like hell I was going to leave her now, not when she was so close to coming back. What if my presence was helping her?

Then again, what if my presence was making her worse? I didn't want to think about that one.

Bird got up slowly and placed his hand on my shoulder. "I know you care about her. But she's not going anywhere for now. We have to cleanse the room. Then you can come back in."

Roman said something to Bird in the native language and Bird nodded sharply before looking back me. "Please? We must hurry."

I couldn't argue with Bird. With a sigh, Ada and I left the room together. We gave Perry one last look, trying to tell her we'd be back to fight with her, before Bird closed the door on us.

EIGHT

WE WEREN'T REALLY SURE WHERE TO GO, WHAT TO DO. Ada leaned against the door, trying to hear what was going on but I went down the hall and flopped down on Roman's sagging couch, the springs creaking under me. There was no way I could listen to what was going on inside, without knowing exactly what it was. It would be too painful to make my own conclusions in the dark. I could only put what little faith I had left into Bird. I had to hope for the best. I had to have hope, even when hope seemed impossible, eaten away by the darkest monster.

Eventually, Ada came over. She sat beside me and put her head in her hands. I rubbed her back lightly, not sure if there was even a point in trying to comfort her. I sure as hell couldn't be.

"What does it sound like?" I asked.

She shrugged. "Nothing too bad. I don't hear Perry, just Roman and Bird chanting some stuff."

I nodded, glad it wasn't worse. I fished some Nicorette out of my pocket and popped the last two pieces in my mouth, chewing away like it was going to save my sanity.

We didn't say much to each other. There was nothing we really could say. Talking seemed futile. Thinking seemed useless. I just stared over her white-blonde head and out the hole-covered screen door, to the back yard that seemed to stretch on forever in hills of dust and light. Yesterday I had been having pizza with Rebecca, thinking I'd never see Perry again. Now, I was with her, but her soul was far away. It didn't seem fair. It didn't seem easy. All the back and forth between us, all our struggles with each other and with ourselves and we still weren't fixed. We were still both terribly broken, and for once, it seemed like Perry was the one beyond repair.

After what seemed like forever, Roman opened the door and stuck his head out into the hall.

"You can come back in now," he said, retreating back inside.

Ada and I exchanged an anxious glance and got to our feet. The room now was completely black with the shades drawn tight and a bunch of smelly smoke lingered in the air.

Ada coughed and waved it away from her face.

But Roman was quick. "No," he said, firmly grabbing Ada's hand in mid-wave. "Don't move it. It is to help us. Breathe it in. It will help purify you both."

I did as he said, hoping that a lungful of sage and whatever else it was would be as good for me as a cigarette. Christ, I could have killed for one.

He shut the door behind us and told us to stand at the foot of the bed. We both approached Perry with trepidation as he went to the other side of her. She looked no worse than before, but also no better.

Roman kept his eyes on Perry as he said to us, "Tell me how this all started."

I gave Ada a look. I was a late party to this whole thing.

She nodded, knowing it was her responsibility, and stepped closer to Roman, going over everything that happened from the start. It hurt to hear it all over again.

When she was done, Roman turned to me.

"And where do you come in?"

I cleared my throat, feeling like an idiot for being on the outside. "The little one called me. I was the only one who believed what was wrong with Perry."

"What was Perry's state of mind before all of this happened?"

I opened my mouth but had no idea what to say. How was Perry? How did I leave her? She had been ruined, just like me. We'd ruined each other and left the other one for dead.

Ada was watching me, her blue eyes sparkling hotly. She was *not* amused.

"Perry's state of mind?" Ada repeated. "She was emo as shit."

Yeah, it was going to take a while before I was out of the doghouse.

Ada came up to me and stuck her pointy finger underneath my chin, her nail digging in uncomfortably. "This asshole broke up with Perry. Broke her poor fucking heart right in two. I'm only tolerating him because he was the last chance we had."

Right. So now I knew it for sure. She was relying on me because she had to. She dug her finger in deeper, emphasizing her point, and my eyes went to the floor. Shame didn't quite explain it. She thought this was all my fault. Everyone now knew this was all my fault. The floor seemed to wave underneath my gaze but maybe that was the water in my eyes.

"I see," Roman said slowly and with a heavy sigh.

"Yeah," Ada continued, "basically slept with her and ditched her, used her..."

"Hey, okay, wait a minute," I said, stepping away from her lethal tips. "That's not exactly what happened."

She glared at me with all the condemnation a teenage girl could muster (which, by the way, is a lot). "Oh yeah, perhaps you better explain what happened. Why Perry cried in her room for days wondering what the hell went wrong. You weren't there. You didn't have to help her day in and out, hoping that one day she'd come out of it and realize what a goddamn asshole you are. You didn't see the way you left her. You didn't have to help her pick up the pieces."

She looked at Roman with persuasion. "Plus, there was the whole him getting her pregnant and miscarriage thing."

Boom.

I was sucker punched right in the heart. Right in the motherfucking heart. It stopped. My lungs stopped. Everything stopped, hanging in the room with those words.

Miscarriage.

Pregnant.

Miscarriage.

Pregnant.

I had gotten Perry pregnant? I...I...no...

No. It couldn't be.

I brought my eyes to Perry and saw her there. Saw her sadness. Saw her truth.

There were no words. There was nothing.

I had gotten her pregnant. She had been pregnant with my child.

For two seconds my heart could have burst with such happy heat. For the unimaginable, undeserving, unbelievable concept that Perry had a life inside of her that was both hers and mine. The one thing I'd always wanted but never dared to dream. It had happened. It was ours.

Once.

My heart shrank. Because she'd lost the baby. She'd lost it. What was ours. What was love. What was life.

There was pain and then there was agony.

Hello, agony. I'd been waiting for you. Finish me off. Please.

"You didn't know," Roman said as he stared at me, stating the obvious.

I looked away from Perry's eyes, not wanting her to see me like this. Ada placed her hand on my shoulder. "Hey, sorry. I'm sorry."

I shrugged her hand off, unable to breathe, unable to think. "I need to get some air."

"No," Roman commanded. "You're not going. We have to discuss this, all of this. It will help me figure out what happened. What's in her."

"What's in her?" I glared at him. Wasn't it obvious? "A demon, that's what."

Roman shook his head. "No. You're right, but it's not just that. There are three entities lying there." He pointed over at her. "One is Perry. One is demonic. The other is another entity. It is weak and it has no power anymore. But it is a spirit, a vengeful one. And if my guesses are correct, there was something haunting Perry before. Something that was wronged or ignored. It made a powerful pact, deal if you will, to gain Perry's soul. But was lost before it could even happen."

He looked to Ada. "And this miscarriage. Perry would have been at her lowest, most vulnerable. It's times like that, or pregnancy, when something foreign can grow and latch on with the baby. Even if the baby was eventually lost. Though you can bet it was because of this spirit."

At the mention of *baby*, my lungs felt kicked. I turned through the smoky haze and leaned against the wall, trying to keep myself from disintegrating right there and then. Perry had been pregnant and it was ripped from her. Just the right time for someone else to move on in. And I knew who it was. I should have known all this time.

"It was Abby," I said, choking on my words. Roman appeared beside me, puzzled.

I explained, "She was haunting me when Perry was with me in Seattle. She's an ex…she died. Years ago. But she comes around every now and then. You know, she died because of me. And I don't think she'll ever forget it."

Abby. As if this couldn't be more of my fault. I got Perry pregnant, I hurt her deeply, then my dead ex-girlfriend decided she wasn't done. When I was younger and at the mercy of my mother, hiding from her while she searched for me in a drunken rage, I often wished I was someone else. And when she died—at my own hands—I thought Declan Foray O'Shea was the biggest waste of space that this planet had ever seen. But now…now I wished I hadn't been born at all. It would have saved us all a lot of trouble.

"She will now," Roman said, his voice hard. "The demon gained access to Perry through her, played on her fears through her. To get to you. This spirit is no more. Demons don't keep their bargains."

I shook my head. "So that's it. It has one ex-girlfriend of mine. And it's not satisfied. It wants the only person left on this earth that I…that I'd do *anything* for. Just throw her into the pot, who cares. I lost her once, I cannot lose her again."

"Life is unfair for a lot of people and for a lot of reasons,"

Bird spoke up quietly. "This isn't about you Dex, though I know from experience your intentions are good. This is about Perry. This is about what we can do to help her. We can't waste time placing blame on each other or being angry. That's what it wants. We need to help her. And we need to hurry. You can deal with everything else afterward."

It was hard to listen. It was hard to know that Bird was right. That it wasn't about me. It wasn't about my feelings, my guilt, my problems, my shame. It was about Perry. I was here to save her, or die trying. And I wasn't dead yet.

I turned around and faced the room, not caring if they saw the tears in my eyes. I only cared about one thing. Make that two things.

I walked over to Ada and stuck out my hand. "I'm extremely, unrelentingly sorry for what I did to your sister. To Perry. And, by default, to you. Little Fifteen."

Ada looked at my hand like it was covered in herpes. Then she gave me a small smile and shook my hand. It gave me strength.

"Good," Roman said, looking us over. "We need a united front against this. Even with Bird acting as my helper, I will need you both to be strong and to have no fear. You have to believe that we can beat it. We are superior to this beast and we will get it out. But you must have conviction in your beliefs. To doubt is to endanger all of our lives, and especially Perry's."

Bird began to drum lightly while Roman brought up a small wooden bowl from the floor. He took it over to Perry, his eyes ruthlessly cutting into her, looking for the monster underneath.

"And so we begin the sacred ceremony," he announced. "An exorcism is a battle. I will lead it until the end."

He raised up the bowl and started yelling in his native

tongue, short and sharp words that seemed to sink into you like rain, tangible and real.

Perry immediately reacted. She began writhing back and forth underneath the straps, panting hard like a wild beast. Motherfucking steam rose from her body, giving me the chills. What the shit was happening?

Roman was relentless. He was fueled by the beast's misery, by Perry's agonizing reaction. It was hard to watch but I couldn't look away, no matter how hard I tried. The floor, Ada's tortured face, Bird's steady drumming; I kept being drawn back to Perry, like she wanted me to watch. Like it helped in some way.

Roman paused and dipped his thumbs into the wooden bowl until they were blackened with soot, then approached her. She flung her head back and forth, trying to escape his hands but he succeeded in getting one swipe down her cheek.

Then she bit him on the hand.

I cried out as the blood ran down her chin. I couldn't help it. To say I was horrified was an understatement

But I wasn't the one doing the exorcist. Roman didn't seem to feel any terror. He jabbed an ink-black thumb straight into Perry's forehead and her head flew back from the force, letting go of his hand, which he calmly took back.

The monster smiled, bloody teeth, bloody lips, bloody gums. Perry was completely gone. And as if it needed to hammer that point right on home, it spoke through her, in a voice that I'd never forget. A voice straight out of the earth, omnipresent and overpowering.

"Think she'll be so lucky this time? After what you did to little Jim?"

It was loud and malevolent. I was sure the ground was going to open up beneath us and we would fall into the fiery pits of hell. This couldn't be real. After everything I had seen so far, even in the last twenty-four hours, it still couldn't be real.

But it was.

And Roman, bless his crazy ass soul, he was not phased. He kept repeating his words, his voice becoming stronger, clearer. She started screaming and banging the back of her head against the mattress, making Linda Blair's performance in *The Exorcist* look like a mere temper tantrum.

Everything got louder, so damn intense. Perry was covered in sweat and started to slide out from under the straps.

"Dex, Ada!" Roman yelled. "Get a hold of her legs."

We both rushed forward ready to hold her down but the moment our hands touched her skin, it was like we were grabbing a hot iron.

We quickly let go, my hand inflamed and red. She was a hundred degrees.

"She's burning hot!" I cried out. "You're killing her!"

"Do it!" Roman yelled. And maybe the power of Christ compelled me or something, but I went back. I grabbed her leg, holding her down, wincing through the pain as my skin singed from the contact.

"United front, Dex," Roman said through gritted teeth. "You can't let your feelings get in the way. We must do this. You too, Ada."

Ada sniffled in response, obeying him through her tears. It was killing her inside to do this to Perry, as much as it was killing any of us.

And the monster inside Perry wasn't done with us yet.

"You killed him. The mother killed herself shortly after. You ruined a town," the monster seethed out through Perry.

"You'll ruin her. I will ruin her. You are powerless, foolish and weak."

She burst into haunting laughter that tore through me, seeming to come from the walls, the floor, the air. She was everywhere.

"You can do what you want to her," Roman said forcefully, "but I am stronger and I will win this battle. I will get you out and send you back to where you came from."

Oh shit, I hoped Roman was confident enough in his abilities, because it felt like my fingers were melding in with Perry's skin. I felt like time wasn't on our side anymore and this was only going to get worse.

Suddenly the area around the bed erupted in flames that rose from the floor in a thick line, nearly engulfing us. Ada and I stumbled back, running from the fire. Even Bird stopped drumming, stunned by what was happening.

"Keep going!" Roman screamed at Bird over the roar of the flames.

Bird snapped to it and continued, his hands slapping steadily on the drum.

The flames grew higher until they provided a barricade between us and Perry. I held Ada tight to my side as she trembled, both of us now a captive audience.

In one swift, violent motion, Perry sat straight up, breaking the straps around her arms. She grinned at Roman and in a most disturbing voice of a little boy, "Why did you have to be so rough? You hurt me. You broke my bones."

"No!" Roman yelled, and then bellowed a string of harsh-sounding native words.

"Yes, you did," the voice continued, teasingly, like a child on the playground. "You broke me in a million pieces. You told me you had to hurt me to free me."

Roman kept reciting his mantra over and over again,

watching Perry like his eyes were glued to her, never breaking, never faltering.

"And you," she said, turning her head to look at me.

"Let's not forget what you did, Declan."

But it wasn't her who spoke. It was my mother's voice.

She was here.

My arm came off of Ada and I was afraid I was going to die of fright right there.

Perry—my *mother*—laughed, so familiar, so terrible. "Your little secret. You don't want anyone to know about what happened to your dear old mother. I'm in here now. In here with your little tramp. And I will do to her what you did to me."

No.

She would not expose my secret. She would *not* take my Perry.

Suddenly the rest of the straps broke in two and she went flying backward as if booted by an invisible force, her head smacking the wall with a sickening crack.

Next thing I knew there I was screaming and burning alive. I'd tried to run through the fire, to get to her, to save her from my mother but I couldn't make it. The flames engulfed me, swallowing me from head to toe. I was sure I was a goner but someone pulled me back and shoved me to the ground where I rolled. Through all of this I could hear Perry's head being thrown against the wall.

"Dex!" Roman yelled above the noise. "It's testing you, don't listen to it. It wants your fear, it feeds on it!"

Then it must have been having the feast of a lifetime. I shrugged off my jacket, which was somehow only lightly singed, and Ada helped me to my feet. Her attention was elsewhere though. Everyone's was.

Perry was now floating right above us, her back on the

ceiling, staring down at us as the flames roared around the bed. She laughed and laughed and laughed and we were at her mercy.

"I will do to her what you did to me," and this time, it was Abby's voice that came out.

She was back. She was going to take Perry somewhere far away. Somewhere to feast on her soul. Perry's beautiful, precious soul. And she'd kill her body in the process. She'd leave behind no trace of the girl I knew and loved. Oh god, I loved her.

This wasn't what I came here to do. I came here to save her. And if it wasn't Roman who could do it, it had to be me. The world was better for having her soul in it.

I looked Roman in the eyes and yelled at him, "Take me! Let it take me. It needs a soul, it can have mine!"

But the bastard ignored me and shook his head. "I can win this battle."

"No, you can't," the monster replied through Perry's lips. "You can't win. I'll kill her before you even get a chance. Then I'll take him."

It smiled sweetly at me.

And then she fell.

NINE

The minute she hit the ground, I was sure she was dead. But she immediately started moving, just tossing and turning on the ground like she was having a seizure. There was no demon in sight but there was no Perry either.

"What's happening?" Ada cried as Bird and Roman tried to hold her still, Bird cupping her face and head as gently as he could. I fell to my knees and tried to touch her, but she writhed away from under my fingers.

"I don't know," Roman said. Not the words I wanted to hear. But before I could do or say anything, Perry was suddenly ripped from their hands. She zoomed to the center of the room where she floated, suspended in the air, lifeless except for an ultraviolet light that shone out from her center, like she was some god awful sun.

We watched her, frozen on the spot. She just hung there in the air and when Roman went to go touch her, he was mildly shocked by some kind of energy.

He licked his lips nervously. "She's in another place."

My eyes widened. "What other place?"

He shook his head and took a step forward. "We can't

reach her in the physical anymore. Bird, I need you to continue."

Bird snapped to life and brought the drums to him, sitting beside me as I sat back on my knees. The drumming began, rhythmic and powerful. Roman raised his arms wide and started chanting again, yelling and sputtering, sounding less confident by the minute. Ada remained by the wall, shaking like a leaf, crying her eyes out. I wanted to comfort her but there was nothing to say. I needed comfort too.

"What other place?" I repeated.

Roman went on, shouting louder and louder at the bright and terrible light. Sweat fell off him in rivets. He was losing it and losing the battle.

"Roman!" I screamed. "What other place?"

"The Thin Veil," he snapped, his cool demeanor shot. "Where the spirits wait. She's there now. I don't think we can get her back."

"You don't think?" I asked in horror. "You don't have a choice. You said you could fix her!"

"Actually I said I couldn't!" he yelled back. "I can't reach her. It won't let me in."

"But it'll let me in!" I found myself saying.

He gave me an odd look, half his face whited-out by Perry's never-ending glow.

I went on, feeling I finally knew something, that I could do the thing I set out to do. Save her. "It wants me, it practically said so. Let me reach her. Put me in a trance, do whatever you need to do to send me to her. It will let me in. Let me help. You can reach her through me. Use me."

This time Bird spoke up. "You can't risk it. The pathway doesn't work like that. If you find her and free her, it may take you instead."

"Then it's worth it," I said determinedly.

"There will be many times you may have to lay your life on the line for her. You must choose your battles wisely, Dex. You can only give up your life once."

"Let him do it," Roman said quietly. "If this is his wish, I can use him to find her. I can bring her out. I can keep both of them safe."

"No you can't," Bird said.

"Dex is right," Roman argued. "There is no other way."

He turned away from Perry and stood above me.

"Are you sure you want to do this Dex?" he asked. He looked a million years old, a million years defeated.

I nodded. "I've never been so sure of anything in my whole life."

"Then may your conviction help you find her," he said. He placed his hand on my forehead and my eyes immediately closed from the heat of his palm.

"Think of her and only her. Call for her. Look for her. Make her come back," he said. I could feel waves of energy flowing from him to me. He moved away slightly and I knew he was grabbing Perry's hand as she hung in the air.

The light in my head flashed white and faded.

"Find her," Roman's voice echoed and then was gone.

I opened my eyes. It was completely black. I couldn't see a thing but maybe there was nothing to see.

I looked down, unsure if I had a body, unsure if I could feel. Could I move?

"Perry," I called out, trying to focus my thoughts on her, trying to will her into my new existence. I thought about moving forward and cold wind rushed past. The black opened up to grey. My body began to take shape below me. I was translucent, like a ghost.

"Perry," I called out again. I needed to find her. Where was she?

I wandered in the grey nothingness for who knows how long. Minutes? An eternity?

But, finally, I heard her. I felt her.

"Dex," she said, like the sweetest word on earth.

I turned around and saw her right behind me.

She glowed like an angel, her face a radiant alabaster, her lips red and full, her eyes so vivid that they seized me, holding me breathless. My smile nearly broke my face in two.

I reached out for her hand, to bring her to me, to take her back. But it only passed through her. I really was the ghost here. Only she was solid.

"I don't understand," I said, shaking my head. "Why can't I touch you?"

I went for her shoulder but the same thing happened. My hand disintegrated as it passed through her. She was there but I was not. I couldn't feel her at all. Why couldn't I feel her? How could I save her now?

"I don't know," she said, her eyes widening in panic. "What's happening to you, how are you here?"

"Roman has got a hold on both of us. I just thought of you until I…until I saw you. Here. Wherever this is." I looked around at the limitless grey. "But I don't think I'm here enough."

I reached for her face, trying to make my fingers solid, trying so desperately to touch her. Was I not enough? Would I fail in the end, leaving Perry here alone? It couldn't end this way. It wouldn't. It wouldn't.

I searched her eyes, trying to connect, trying to bring us together, trying to make us real. I needed to save her. I needed to save us.

But my fingers still passed through her, as hers went

through me. In the distance, wherever the distance was, something rumbled, low and evil.

"I think it's coming," I whispered. It saw us. It knew I was here. The monster that had her body but did not yet have her soul. I closed my eyes. "I need to take you back with me. I can't leave you here."

"I know," she said. "Concentrate."

"I am." The desperation was ripping apart my heart. I put every thought directed toward her. I thought about the first time I saw her in the lighthouse, how I saw that fire inside of her, how it took my breath away, how I wanted her. I thought about our first slow dance to Billy Joel in Red Fox, thinking, knowing, needing her to be mine. I thought about the taste of her as we kissed in that tent on D'Arcy Island, the feel of her body. I thought about the first time I realized I loved her, the first time I made love to her, feeling her from the inside. I thought about breaking her heart and breaking my own and needing her more than I've ever needed anyone. I thought about all this darkness and how she'd always be my light.

"You have to get out of here," she whispered. "Go back."

"Not without you," I told her.

"We both can't stay here," she pleaded. "You must go."

"Roman is growing weaker," I said. *He wouldn't be able to get you back*, is what I was too afraid to say.

"So, please go!" she cried.

But I wouldn't. I'd gladly die there with her. Always with her.

I tried to put my hand on her face. "Will you forgive me?"

She was startled. "What?"

"For all the things I've done to you. Will you forgive

me?" It was all I needed to find peace in myself. To have the mercy in her.

"Of course," she whispered.

I smiled as a breeze whirled around us. My soul felt like it had wings.

I kissed her, as much as I could.

Our hearts are magnets, I heard her voice come into my head, a voice she never spoke. I heard her thoughts, pure and powerful.

And with that, I felt *everything*. Her soft lips under mine, her tongue, her warmth. Everything that was Perry. I grabbed onto her as hard as I could, vowing to never ever let go and she returned the favor, wrapping her arms around my waist. Suddenly, we were flying back through the air, like we were pulled by a chord. But we were together, wherever we were going.

Then it stopped. The darkness melted into light. I felt Perry fall from my arms and Roman's hand fall from my head. I was back in my body, back in the world.

And Perry was right beside me, kneeling on the carpet, alive but well, Roman connecting the two of us.

"Your soul is yours," Roman said to both of us, his voice dropping with exhaustion.

We both slumped to the floor in peace.

THERE'S NOTHING LIKE GOING TO ANOTHER DIMENSION to make you tired as fuck. When I woke up from the aftermath a few hours later, I felt like every bone in my body had been broken and my head had been presented with the world's largest hangover. It was worse than the time I drank a bottle of Baja Rosa and a liter of wine (hey, it was college).

Perry was still under, snoring away, which was a good sign. Her little nose was cute when she did that. It was a reminder that she was herself again. Roman said she'd be sleeping for a day but when she came to, most of her injuries from the ceremony would be healed. He said because they'd happened in another world, at least from a being from another world, that she'd be okay. She'd certainly seen better days but at least she was whole again.

As for me, well my head still hurt a bit from the car accident and my favorite jacket was singed to shit, but I was okay. I mean, yeah there was the whole feeling like shit thing, but I'd get over that. I felt amazing deep inside, knowing I'd saved her or at least helped. I didn't feel like I'd made anything even between us and I didn't know if she'd even want to talk to me despite everything I did, but I didn't care. She could spit on my face and kick me in the balls and I would still love it because she was alive and well. A world without Perry Palomino is just too fucking boring. I wouldn't wish it upon anyone.

Ada was obviously over the moon but the poor kid was so shell-shocked that it was taking her a while to come around. I think she was so afraid of the entity coming back, even though she had no reason to be. It was hard to explain, but I just knew it was gone and it wouldn't return. At least not for her.

And I knew Roman felt the same way. He'd been sleeping on and off, trying to work his way through the terrible strain he'd been under. But it had to be somewhat cathartic to know that he'd finally won. Sure, I went in there in the end like the fucking action hero I always wanted to be, but I couldn't have saved her without Roman there. He took a chance on me, on Perry, and I would be forever in his debt for it.

That night, we put Perry on a small bed in Roman's study. Though there was no room for me to lie with her, I did what I could. I had her back, even in her unconscious state, and we weren't going to be apart for a minute, not if I could help it. If that made me overprotective, so be it. I was going to protect this woman—my woman—until the day I died.

I stayed up with her as long as I could keep my eyes open. It was morning when she stirred enough that I knew she was well. She muttered, "Dex," once in her sleep, then smiled to herself and drifted off again. I felt like I was on top of the fucking world.

Before I settled down into the pillows Roman had thrown along the side of the bed, my makeshift mattress, I took Perry's hand in mine and held it up to my lips, peering over her. She looked like an angel lying there as dawn broke somewhere on the horizon, bathing the room in an ethereal glow.

"You're my light in all this madness, Perry," I whispered, knowing she couldn't hear me. "It all fades away when I'm with you. Everything fades until it's just you and it's just me. I'm Dex and you're Perry and I love you. I won't stop loving you, even when you won't love me. I love you more than I can ever really tell you. I love you until the end."

I felt myself choking on my tears a bit while I kissed her hand. I kissed her soft forehead. Then I peeled back the blanket and gently touched her middle, watching her serene face as sleep still held her so close.

I smiled though she couldn't see it and placed my lips on her stomach. "I would have loved the baby too, more than you'll ever know."

Then I pulled away, and still holding her hand tightly,

lay down on the ground beside her. I held her, even as the darkness took me away.

ABOUT THE AUTHOR

Karina Halle, a former screenwriter, travel writer and music journalist, is the *New York Times*, *Wall Street Journal*, and *USA Today* bestselling author of *The Pact*, *A Nordic King*, and *Sins & Needles*, as well as over fifty other wild and romantic reads. She, her husband, and their adopted pit bull live in a rain forest on an island off British Columbia, where they operate a B&B that's perfect for writers' retreats. In the winter, you can often find them in California or on their beloved island of Kauai, soaking up as much sun (and getting as much inspiration) as possible. For more information, visit

www.authorkarinahalle.com

ALSO BY KARINA HALLE

Contemporary Romances

Love, in English

Love, in Spanish

Where Sea Meets Sky (from Atria Books)

Racing the Sun (from Atria Books)

The Pact

The Offer

The Play

Winter Wishes

The Lie

The Debt

Smut

Heat Wave

Before I Ever Met You

After All

Rocked Up

Wild Card (North Ridge #1)

Maverick (North Ridge #2)

Hot Shot (North Ridge #3)

Bad at Love

The Swedish Prince

The Wild Heir

A Nordic King

Nothing Personal

My Life in Shambles

Discretion

Disarm

Disavow

The Royal Rogue

The Forbidden Man

Lovewrecked

One Hot Italian Summer

The One That Got Away

All the Love in the World (Anthology)

Romantic Suspense Novels by Karina Halle

Sins and Needles (The Artists Trilogy #1)

On Every Street (An Artists Trilogy Novella #0.5)

Shooting Scars (The Artists Trilogy #2)

Bold Tricks (The Artists Trilogy #3)

Dirty Angels (Dirty Angels #1)

Dirty Deeds (Dirty Angels #2)

Dirty Promises (Dirty Angels #3)

Black Hearts (Sins Duet #1)

Dirty Souls (Sins Duet #2)

Horror Romance

Darkhouse (EIT #1)

Red Fox (EIT #2)

The Benson (EIT #2.5)

Dead Sky Morning (EIT #3)

Lying Season (EIT #4)

On Demon Wings (EIT #5)

Old Blood (EIT #5.5)

The Dex-Files (EIT #5.7)

Into the Hollow (EIT #6)

And With Madness Comes the Light (EIT #6.5)

Come Alive (EIT #7)

Ashes to Ashes (EIT #8)

Dust to Dust (EIT #9)

Ghosted (EIT #9.5)

Came Back Haunted (EIT #10)

The Devil's Duology

Donners of the Dead

Veiled

Made in United States
North Haven, CT
31 March 2025